WITHERING HOPE

LAYLA HAGEN

Published: Layla Hagen 2015
Interior Layout by Author's HQ
Cover Design: by Ari at Cover it! Designs
Proofreading by Allyson Whipple

Other Books Available By Layla Hagen

The Lost Series

Lost: prequel-James and Serena's story

Lost in Us: James and Serena's story

Found in Us: Parker and Jessica's story

Caught in Us: Dani and tattoo guy's story – Spring 2015

Chapter 1

Aimee

My last flight as Aimee Myller starts like any other flight: with a jolt.

I lean my head on the leather headrest, closing my eyes as the private jet takes off. The ascent is smooth, but my stomach still tightens the way it always does during take-offs. I keep my eyes closed for a little while even after the plane is level. When I open up my eyes, I smile. Hanging over the seat in front of me, inside a cream-colored protection bag, is the world's most beautiful wedding dress.

My dress.

It does wonders for me, giving my boyish figure curves. I'll be wearing it in exactly one week. The wedding will take place at my fiancé Chris's gorgeous vacation ranch in Brazil, where I'm heading right now. I've made this flight numerous times before, but it's the first time I'm traveling in Chris's private six-passenger jet without him, and it feels empty.

When I next board this plane, my last name will be Moore, Mrs. Christopher Moore. I sink farther down in my seat, enjoying the feeling of smooth leather on my skin. The emptiness of the plane is accentuated by the fact that there is no flight attendant tonight.

I couldn't bring myself to ask Kyra, Chris's flight attendant, to work tonight. Her daughter turned three today, and she's had the party planned for ages. No reason for her to pay because I decide on a whim that I absolutely have to return to the ranch tonight instead of tomorrow so I can supervise the wedding preparations.

The poor pilot, Tristan, wasn't so lucky—he had to give up what would have been a free night. But he'll forgive me. I've found people are willing to forgive many things—too many in my opinion—from a future bride. I'll have to find a way to make it up to Tristan. Maybe I'll buy him something he'll enjoy as a token of gratitude. That might be a challenge since I don't know Tristan all that well, though he's been working for Chris for a few years. Tristan is very guarded.

I've gotten pretty close to Kyra, who seems beside herself whenever I travel on the plane. I suspect Chris and the business partners he usually flies with aren't as entertaining as the endless discussions we have about the wedding. But all I have managed with Tristan is to get him to talk to me on a first name basis and crack an occasional joke.

Three hours into the flight, Tristan's voice resounds through the speakers. "It looks like there will be more turbulence than usual tonight. It'll be safest if you don't leave your seat for the next hour.

And keep your seatbelt fastened."

"Got it," I say, then remember he can't hear me.

The plane starts jolting vigorously soon after that, but I don't worry too much. Tristan Bress is an excellent pilot, even though he's only twenty-eight—just two years older than I am. I've made this flight often enough. I'm almost used to the occasional turbulences. Almost.

I peek out the window and see we are flying over the Amazon rainforest. The mass of green below is so vast it gives me goose bumps. I gulp. Even though I'm not scared, the continuous jolts do affect me. An unpleasant nausea starts at the back of my throat, and my stomach rolls, somersaulting with each brusque movement of the plane. I check the seat in front of me for the sick bag. It's there.

I grip the hem of my white shirt with both hands in an attempt to calm myself. It doesn't work; my fingers are still twitching. I put my hands in the pockets of my jeans and try to focus on the wedding. That brings a smile to my face. Everything will be perfect. Well, almost everything. I wish my parents could be with me on my wedding day, but I lost them both eight years ago, just before starting college. I close my eyes, trying to block the nausea. After a few minutes it works. Even though the flight isn't one bit smoother, my anxiety loosens a bit.

And then an entirely new kind of anxiety grips me.

The plane starts losing height. My eyes fly open. As if on cue, Tristan's voice fills the cabin. "I have to descend to a lower altitude. We'll get back up as soon as possible. You have nothing to worry about."

An uneasy feeling starts forming inside me. This

hasn't happened before. Still, I have full confidence in Tristan's abilities. There is no reason to worry, so I do my best not to. Until a deafening sound comes from outside. I snap my head in that direction. At first I see nothing except my own reflection in the window: green eyes and light brown, shoulder-length hair. Then I press my forehead to the window. What I see outside freezes the air in my lungs. In the dim twilight, smoke paints black clouds in front of my window.

Black smoke swirls from the one and only engine of the plane.

"Aimee," Tristan's voice says calmly, "I would like you to bend forward and hug your knees. Hurry." The measured tone with which he utters each word scares me like nothing else. "We've lost our engine and I am starting the procedure for an emergency landing."

I barely have time to panic, let alone move, when the plane gives such a horrendous jolt that I bang my head on the window. A sharp pain pierces my temple, and a cry escapes from deep in my throat. Sharper pain follows. Piercing. Raw.

My body seems to have moved on its own, because I'm bent over, hugging my knees. Horrible thoughts wiggle their way into my mind. *Emergency landing*. What percentage of emergency landings go well? My heart races so frantically, and the plane drops so fast it's impossible to imagine it's very high. Another thought grips me. Where will we land? We were over the rainforest last I looked. We couldn't have made it very far since then. My palms sweat, and I grit my teeth as the plane inclines, feeling like I'll be ripped from my seat and propelled forward.

The temptation to raise my head to look out the window is suffocating. I want to know where we are, when the inevitable impact will arrive. But I can't move, no matter how much I try. I'm not sure if it's the plane's position forcing me to stay down or the fear. I tilt my head to one side, facing the corridor. The sight of the protective bag with the dress inside sprawled on the floor makes me forget my fear for a moment, leaving one thought stand out. Chris. My wonderful fiancé, who I have known since I was a small child and with whom I practically grew up. With his round, blue eyes and stubborn blond curls, he still looks boyish, even at the age of twenty-seven and dressed in expensive suits.

I'm thinking about him when the crash comes.

Chapter 2

Aimee

I wake up covered in cold sweat and something soft that might be a blanket. I can't tell for sure, because when I open my eyes, it's dark. When I try to move, a sharp pain in my temple makes me gasp.

"Aimee?"

"Tristan." The word comes out almost like a cry. In the faint moonlight coming in through the windows, I see him leaning on the seat in front of me, hovering over me. I imagine his dark brown eyes searching me worriedly.

"Are you hurt?"

"Just my temple, but I'm not bleeding," I say, running my fingers over the tender spot. I assess him next. It's difficult given the dim moonlight. His white uniform shirt is smeared with dirt, but he appears unharmed. I turn my head toward the window. I can't gauge anything outside in the darkness.

"Where are we?" I ask.

"We landed," Tristan says simply, and when I

turn to look at him he adds, "... in the rainforest."

I nod, trying not to let the tight knot of fear in my chest overtake me. If I let it spiral out, I may not be able to control it.

"Shouldn't we ... like... leave the plane or something? Until they rescue us? Is it safe for us to be inside?"

Tristan runs a hand through his short, black hair. "Trust me, this is the *only* safe place. I checked outside for any fuel leaks, but we're good."

"You got out?" I whisper.

"Yes."

"I want—" I say, opening my seatbelt and trying to stand. But dizziness forces me back into my chair.

"No," Tristan says, and he slumps in the seat opposite mine on the other side of the slim aisle. "Listen to me. You need to calm down."

"How deep in the forest are we, Tristan?"

He leans back, answering after a long pause. "Deep enough."

"How will they find us?" I curl my knees to my chest under the blanket, the dizziness growing. I wonder when Tristan put the blanket over me.

"They will," Tristan says.

"But there is something we can do to make it easier for them, isn't there?"

"Right now, there isn't."

"Can we contact someone at base?" I ask weakly.

"No. We lost all communication a while ago." His shoulders slump, and even in the moonlight, I notice his features tighten. His high cheekbones, which usually give him a noble appearance, now make him look gaunt. Yet instead of panic, I'm engulfed in weakness. My limbs feel heavy. Fog settles over my mind.

"What happened to the engine?" I whisper.

"Engine failure."

"Can you repair it?"

"No."

"There is really no way to send anyone a message?"

"No." As if in a dream, I feel Tristan put a pillow under my head and recline my seat.

I close my eyes, drifting away, thinking of Chris again. Of how worried he must be.

Chapter 3

Aimee

It's daytime when I open my eyes; weak sun rays illuminate the plane. I've slept with my head in an uncomfortable position, and it's given me a stiff neck. I massage my neck for a few minutes, looking around for Tristan, but he isn't anywhere in sight. I try to breathe in, but the air is thick and heavy, and I end up choking. Desperate for fresh air, I look up and discover the door at the front of the plane is open. So Tristan must be outside. I stand slowly, afraid the dizziness from last night might return. It doesn't. I avoid looking out the windows as I walk through the aisle between the two rows of seats, running my hands on the armrests of the three seats on each side. If I'm about to have the shock of my life, I prefer to face it all at once, through the door, not snippet by snippet through the windows.

I stop in front of the door, my eyes still on the ground. The metallic glow of the airstairs—the stairs built into the door of the plane—throws me off for a second. I clench my teeth, pick up my courage, and step forward into the doorway, looking up.

And then I wince.

The view outside the door does not disappoint. It is as terrifying as it is beautiful. Green dominates. The vivid, shiny kind that seems to flow with life. It comes in all shapes and sizes, from lush, dark leaves the size of a tennis racket to the moss covering trees. There is no pattern to the leaves of the trees. Some are heart-shaped, some round. Some spiky, and some unlike anything I have seen before.

Rays of sunlight lance shyly through the thick canopy above us. Trees block a good chunk of the light. Many trees. Tall trees. They tower over us, and I have to lean my head all the way back to see the canopy properly. I frown.

How did Tristan land this plane here unscathed? One look at my right tells me he didn't. I gasp, my grip on the edges of the doorway tightening. The right wing of the plane is a complete wreck. I assume the other wing isn't much better. Two gigantic trees have toppled over the right side of the plane toward the back—with such force they have carved a very deep dent in the plane. Glancing back inside the plane, I see they have fallen right over the only bathroom. I realize with horror the bathroom is probably unusable.

Shuddering, I decide to get out of the plane. When I step off the airstairs, my feet get wet. It must have rained a lot recently, because the ground is fluid mud that engulfs my feet right up to the shoelaces of my running shoes. Each step sloshes, spraying muddy water in every direction as I walk. I inhale deeply. Or at least attempt to. The air is thick with suffocating moisture, but it's not excessively warm. It's been warmer in L.A., where I've lived my whole life. But never this humid. My shirt and jeans have already begun to stick to my damp skin.

"You're up," Tristan says, appearing at the front of the plane. His hands are darkened with dust, and he wipes them with a cloth. His white shirt is unbuttoned at the neck and soaked, molding to his muscular frame. The air seems to get thicker by the minute, and I'd rip open my shirt—or skin—if that would help me breathe better.

"Engine still good?" I ask.

"Still dead, just checked it. There's no risk of anything blowing up; don't worry."

"And the communication system?"

"Also dead. The entire electric system is."

"I know it's unlikely they work here, but how about checking our phones?"

"I checked mine last night after the crash. Yours, too; I hope you don't mind. I found your purse. Your tablet, too. No reception, obviously."

I nod, but the sight of the damaged wing unnerves me, so I turn to look at the jungle instead. The wilderness unnerves me even more.

"Beautiful, isn't it?" he asks.

"I'd prefer to view it on TV. I feel like I've stepped into a documentary."

Tristan steps in front of me, eyeing my cheek. "You have a scratch here. I didn't see it last night. But it's very superficial. Nothing to worry about."

"Oh, well..." I raise my hand to my cheek and my voice trails away as I stare at the diamond engagement ring on my left hand. Chris. The wedding. My beautiful, perfect wedding that should take place in less than a week. I shake my head. It *will* take place. They will rescue us in no time.

"I'm thirsty," I say, turning away from him so he won't see the tears threatening to fill my eyes.

"There are some supplies in the plane. Not much, though. Four cans of soda, which are nothing given the rate at which we'll dehydrate in this climate."

I raise an eyebrow. "We're almost ankle-deep in water. Surely we can find some clever way to have clear water."

"I don't have anything to make a filter good enough to turn this"—he points at the ground— "drinkable. Our best bet is rain."

"How about the water tank in the bathroom?" I ask half-heartedly, thinking of the trees that fell right on top of the bathroom.

"The water tank ruptured—I suspect the moment the trees fell—and the water leaked out."

"Is the bathroom usable at all?" I ask.

"No," Tristan says, confirming my fears. "Everything is wrecked. I crawled inside, and those are the only useful things I could retrieve." He points toward one of the trees that's fallen over the plane. At first I'm confused, but when I look closer I notice there is a pile of what looks like shards of a broken mirror just in front of the tree. "Mirror shards?"

"They are good for signalling our position, among other things."

We both walk toward the pile. I shudder at the sight of the pile of uneven shards. Most are the size of my palm, a few even smaller. If those trees had fallen over my seat, or the cockpit...

I notice there are a few other things lined up next to the mirror shards. A pack of Band-Aids, eye pads, a pair of scissors, a whistle, needles, thread, a pack of insect repellent wipes, and two multifunctional pocket knives.

"These are part of the supplies from the survival kit," Tristan says. "I brought them out to make a quick inventory."

"Why just a part? Where's the other part?"

"Part of the survival kit was in the cockpit. It contained the things you see here. The other part was in a compartment at the back of the plane, next to the bathroom." He gestures toward the point of contact between the fallen trees and the plane. "It was crushed."

"Great." I debate for a second asking him what items were in there but decide against it. Better not to know what we're missing out on.

My stomach rumbles—I'm growing hungry.

"There are also some peanuts, chocolate sticks, and two sandwiches," Tristan says. "Peanuts and chocolate will make the thirst worse, so I suggest avoiding them." The scant supplies don't surprise me. Chris and I flew to the ranch two weeks ago to oversee the final preparations for the wedding. Since he didn't need the jet while at the ranch, he had it sent for its annual technical inspection. A lousy job the technicians did too, considering the crash.

My boss at the law firm I work for unexpectedly asked me to come back to work the third day we were at the ranch, saying he needed help with a case. I flew back to L.A. on a commercial airline. My boss promised it would take less than a week, so I would still have a full week before the wedding to get things ready. The private jet was supposed to take me back, since the inspection would be done by then. I worked day and night, finishing a day early, and told Chris I wanted to return immediately.

The plane had been emptied of all supplies before the technical inspection and was supposed to be restocked the day before taking me to Brazil. Since I insisted on leaving a day earlier than planned, Tristan did some quick supply shopping for this trip.

"We're good," I say. "The supplies should last until they rescue us."

Tristan doesn't answer.

"Won't they last?" I press, turning to him. He's bent on one knee between the pieces of the wrecked wing, inspecting something that separated from the plane and lies on the ground.

"They might last," he says.

"I've read about emergency location transmitters—"

"Ours is defective."

"What?"

"Useless."

"But the plane just had the technical inspection..."

"They did a terrible job," he says angrily.

For a few moments, I am too stunned for words. "The flight plan..." I mumble.

Tristan stands up, his dark brown eyes boring into mine. Somehow I know, even before he opens his mouth, that what he is going to say will kill the last hope I'm clinging to. "We did file a flight plan. But I deviated considerably from it last night when I was looking for a place to land. We lost communication before I deviated, so there was no way I could inform anyone."

"What are you telling me, Tristan?" Desperation

strangles my voice. "That there is no way for them to find us?"

"It's not like that. They can still guess how we—"

"Guess? We're in the middle of—" I stop, looking around wildly. "Where are we? Is the Amazon River nearby?"

"No."

"How do you know?"

"I've climbed that tree to look around." He points at one of the giant trees next to us. "The river isn't anywhere in sight."

"I don't believe that," I whisper. "I don't..." Swirling on my heel, and sinking about an inch further in the muddy earth, I head to the tree.

"What are you doing?" he calls after me.

"I want to see."

"You'll hurt yourself."

"I don't care."

Driven by rabid determination, I curse the overgrown roots around the tree for blocking access to it, but once I find my way through them I'm grateful for them because they help propel me upward until I reach the first branches. I'm not an outdoors girl, and it shows. I'm panting when I'm only halfway up the tree. In my defense, this tree is higher than a three-story house. Once or twice I slip, which may be because I can't bear to look too closely at where I'm putting my hands. The entire surface of the tree is covered with a mushy moss, and by the creepy tingles on my fingers every time I grab a branch, I have the uneasy feeling there are plenty of tiny, multi-legged animals I don't want to see lurking inside it. I've never been a fan of animals with more than four feet.

When I reach the top and wedge myself between two branches, I breathe relieved, happy I made it.

And then I taste bile in my mouth as I take in the sight in front of me. Nothing but green tree-tops. Everywhere. Dense, and stretching as far as I can see. The tree I'm in isn't even high compared to the ones I see in the distance, which makes me think we are on some kind of hill. No sign of the river, or anything that might indicate there are human settlements nearby. If we leave the plane, there is nowhere to go. I make a full turn. From what I can see, in a radius that seems like a few hundred miles, there's no sign of civilization, or a path.

Our best bet is to find the Amazon River and walk alongside it. Human settlements are most likely close to the water. But there's no saying how many miles there are to the river or which direction is the right one. And the jungle isn't a good place to set out on foot, hoping for the best. No... Our hope will have to come from the sky. Which is empty. No planes or helicopters. Not even a distant sound.

A knot forms in my abdomen, and I start another full turn but stop when my head starts spinning. I rest on the branch, closing my eyes. Chris will come looking for me. He will. Determined not to lose my faith, I start climbing down the tree. I cringe as nameless small creatures crawl on my fingers, but I keep my eyes on my destination and manage not to panic.

Until I only have one set of branches between me and the roots, and my hand touches something cold, slimy and far softer than a branch could be. In the fraction of a second it takes me to register it's a snake—a large snake—I instinctively withdraw my hand, which throws me off balance. I hit the roots with a loud thump, landing on my right ankle and twisting it slightly, then stumble forward until Tristan catches me.

"What—?"

"Snake," I mutter, fisting his white shirt, seeking refuge in the warmth of his arms as cold sweat breaks out on every inch of my body. Right. Legless animals have just surpassed multi-legged ones on the list of creatures I despise. Strands of hair stick to my sweaty face, and as I push them away, my engagement ring comes in sight again. And I start crying in earnest, with tears and sobs that wrack my body. As much as I tried to convince myself Chris will find us when I was on top of the tree, down here that seems an impossibility. Tristan is saying something, but I can't make out what.

"I am so glad Kyra isn't with us," I say between sobs.

"Yeah, me too," Tristan says, his arms tightening around me. At least neither Tristan nor I have any children. He has parents, though. Strangely, I feel relieved that my parents aren't alive anymore. I can't imagine what a hell they'd be going through if they knew their only daughter was lost in the Amazon rainforest, most likely dead.

"Chris will do everything to find you, Aimee. Don't doubt that for a second."

"I don't." I say, his words giving me strength. That's true. If I am certain of one thing, it's that Chris will do whatever it takes to find me. Being the heir to his father's multimillion-dollar empire, he has the resources to do it. I don't know how long I stay curled against Tristan, overwhelmed, weak, and sweating. He tries to soothe me, his arms embracing me with an awkwardness groomed over years of spending hours at a time in each other's company, the silence between us interrupted only by polite requests. Our relationship has always been stilted, so different from the relationship I have with the other employees in Chris's household.

Well, his parents' household—the Moore's have an enormous villa with an even more enormous garden just outside L.A. Chris and I live in a spacious apartment downtown with no employees at all. But we're at his parents' house so often, it's almost like a second home. We were there three weeks ago to celebrate my twenty-sixth birthday. Their staff has been with them so long they are like one big family: the cook, the maids, the gardeners, and my beloved Maggie—the woman who cared for Chris and me when we were kids. Our parents were close friends. Since my parents' work took them away from home for months at a time, and Chris and I were the same age, I spent most of my childhood at Chris's home, with Maggie babysitting us.

Chris's parents kept her as housekeeper after we were grown, because she had become like family. I am very close to her and on friendly terms with the other staff. Tristan is the only one who actually works for Chris, flying him around the country about once or twice a week to visit the company's subsidiaries. I see Tristan often, because when Chris doesn't fly out, Tristan is my driver. But we haven't grown any closer because of it.

Still, his presence is like an anchor for me. I rest my head on his hard chest, my cheek pressing against his steel muscles. His heartbeat is remarkably steady. I want his calmness and strength to overpower my despair. I stay in his arms until I've cried out my weakness. Then, with a newly found determination, I stand up.

"Let's walk until we find a river—any river, then we can continue downstream. It must flow into the Amazon. They can find us easier if we're on the river. And if they don't find us," I gulp, "we have a better chance of finding a settlement along a river."

Tristan, his shirt so soaked from the humidity he looks like he's been walking in pouring rain, shakes his head. "For now our best course of action is to stay here, near the plane. It's easier to spot a plane than two people. They might be able to figure out where we crashed. The first forty-eight hours after a crash are when the search missions arc most intense."

Relief ripples along my skin. Forty-eight hours minus the ones when I was knocked out. Then we'll be going home.

"I want to start a fire," I say. "If they send planes over, they will see the fire, right?"

He hesitates. "I doubt they can see a fire down here with the canopy so thick." He's right. The rich canopy weaves itself in a dome above us, allowing slim strings of light to drip through it here and there, drawing loops of light that illuminate the humid cloud-like shadow surrounding us.

"I still want to start a fire."

"We will. There's a way to build it so it's safe even with so many trees nearby. We need a lot of smoke. That'll rise up far above the canopy. It'll be an excellent indicator of our location. It'll be tricky finding dry wood, though. Almost everything here is wet."

"But that's good for smoke, right? Wet wood?"

"Yeah... but we need dry wood to start the fire."

"Can't we start the fire with one of those mirror shards? I don't know much about it, but I saw that on TV once."

"It's not necessary to use a mirror; I have a lighter. But we still need wood."

"We'll find something," I say, undeterred. But Tristan seems hesitant. "What?"

"You stay inside the plane," he says. "I'll search for wood."

"No, I want to be helpful."

"The jungle is a dangerous place, Aimee. I'd rather you were unharmed when Chris finds you. Us."

"Well, if we don't search for the wood, we won't be found. It'll be quicker if we both do it. Besides, we won't go too far away from the plane, will we?"

"No, we won't," Tristan says. "I'll get a can of soda. We have to take care not to dehydrate."

The moment he mentions it, my thirst returns full force, my throat dry and raspy. Tristan disappears inside the plane, returning with a soda. I take the first sip, and it's all I can do not to drink the entire content. I pass the can to him, and he takes a few sips as well.

"Why did you bring just one can?" I say, my throat aching for more.

"We have to be careful not to run out of it."

"But this is the rainforest, right? It should rain soon."

Tristan puts the can on the ground, goes to our supply line-up, and returns with the two pocket knives. "It hasn't rained since we crashed last night. But it's the rainy season; we should have some soon."

"Well, let's look at the bright side, if there's no rain, we can start a fire."

He hands me one of the knives, saying, "Use this to cut any branches that might be useful. Take care where you step."

With that, we head toward the tree nearest to us. It's not the one I climbed earlier. I intend to steer clear of that one, though I'm sure other trees are full of snakes as well. I recoil at the memory of its cold skin. It was a very large snake, though not large enough to be an anaconda. I watched a few documentaries about the Amazon a few weeks back, because our honeymoon was supposed to be in a tourist resort in the rainforest, and Chris wanted to make a safari inside the forest. The documentary told about the millions of things that could kill one in the forest: animals, contaminated water, poisonous food, and a lot more. In fact, the only thing that seemed harmless was the air. It put me off the safari, and I managed to convince Chris to drop it.

Despite being surrounded by trees, finding dry wood turns out to be just as problematic as Tristan predicted. We even search inside hollow trees, but what the rain hasn't touched, condensation has turned unusable for starting a fire. We advance very slowly, the thick plants making our task cumbersome.

"Damn it. If we had a machete this would be easier," Tristan says, walking in front of me. After a while, sweating like a pig, I start losing concentration;

the little soda I drank earlier long having left my body. Tristan appears to be feeling just as bad. The path beneath us slopes slightly downward, which confirms my suspicion we are on a hill. The more we descend, the muddier the ground becomes. It's almost fluid.

"Let's stop for a bit," I pant. I buckle forward, my knees trembling, and I put my hands on my thighs to steady myself. I keep my eyes on the forest floor, which is covered in mud and leaves and has a red hue. I'm grateful I'm wearing running shoes and not sandals, because they protect me from the creatures crawling on the rainforest floor. I notice a myriad of insects, and decide to close my eyes to stop from giving in to panic. But closing my eyes seems to make my ears more sensitive, because the sound of a thousand beings breathing all around me hits me. Angry chirping birds, sinuous slithering, and howling I don't even want to think about. They're ominous, all of them.

"These will do," I hear Tristan say, and with great effort, I stand up straight. He's carrying a bunch of twigs with one arm. "Can you hold these?" I nod and take the twigs from him, holding them tight against my chest with both arms. He returns a few minutes later with another bunch in his arms.

"Are you ready to walk back to the plane, or do you want to rest a while longer?" he asks, eyes full of concern.

"I'm fine, let's go." Tristan puts one of his hands protectively at the small of my back, and I'm grateful, because my legs wobble. My breath skitters as I try to propel my feet forward, and I press the twigs so tight to my chest they crinkle. The walk back takes forever. I pull myself together when I see the plane again. Tristan goes inside and returns with a lighter and a can of soda. We each take a few sips, and I rest against the airstairs, strangely reassured by the feel of the metal against my skin. It's something familiar in this otherwise alien place.

Though overcome by a tiredness that has crept into my bones, I move to help Tristan start the fire, but find he's already done it. He placed it in a spot under a wide hole in the canopy so the smoke can rise high in the sky.

"Lucky you had that lighter," I say, standing next to him.

He smiles. "I can start a fire without a lighter anyway."

"That's an... interesting skill to have." I notice he used all the dry wood to start the fire, and now he's putting the less dry branches on top. Smoke comes in a matter of seconds.

"I must say, after your encounter with the snake, I thought you'd want to avoid the forest," Tristan says.

I chuckle. "Give me some credit, will you?"

He bends over the wood, fumbling with the twigs, rearranging them. Though the fire is weak, swirls of smoke rise up to the sky. They're not strong enough to be visible from a distance though.

"We should gather more wood," I say. "Better wood. We need more smoke."

"No. What we need is water. We have two soda cans left. That's a more pressing issue."

I don't argue. He's right. "Where do you suggest we look for it?" I ask.

Tristan eyes me. "You go inside the plane and

rest for a bit. I'll look for a stream nearby."

"I want to come too."

"No." The firmness in his voice takes me by surprise. "There's no need for both of us to waste our energy."

"I don't want to just stay here, doing nothing."

"Then bring out everything in the plane that can hold water, so if rain comes, we can collect it."

"Got it."

As Tristan leaves, making his way between the trees, armed with his pocket knife, fear grips me. "Be careful," I say.

"Don't worry about me," he calls over his shoulder. There is no tremble in his voice, no hesitation in his steps. The forest doesn't seem to scare him at all. I scout the inside of the plane for anything that might collect water, but I don't find much. I line empty soda cans outside, then start peeking around the wrecked wing to see if there's anything I can use. I scout through the shredded metal, doing my best not to cut myself. No luck. I give up the search when nausea overwhelms me, reminding me my water level is low. I walk over to the airstairs, resting against it. Where is Tristan? How much time has passed since he disappeared into the forest?

I stare at the empty soda cans, when an idea occurs to me. A few trees around me have leaves as huge as a tennis racket. They must be of some use. I drag my feet to one whose leaves have an edge that curls upward, perfect for holding water. I use the pocket knife Tristan gave me to cut the leaves. Though they come off almost effortlessly, by the time I cut off about twelve leaves or so, I feel like

I'm going to faint. I wobble back to the plane, trying to bind the leaves in some form that will hold water. They end up looking like tightly woven baskets. I suppose we'll see if they're tight enough to hold water. I keep my ears strained, hoping to hear a plane fly over us. Nothing.

When I'm done with the leaves, I collapse on the airstairs, exhausted. I'm tempted, oh so tempted to grab another soda can from the plane and drink it...

It's almost dark when Tristan's voice resounds from the trees. "I didn't find anything. Oh, great thinking," he says, pointing to the leaf baskets I laid out in front of me. He looks terrible. His skin is glistening with sweat, and he has dark circles under his eyes. "These should collect a healthy amount of water."

Somewhere in the back of my mind, the implication gnaws at me. We won't leave this place as soon as I thought. But I can't find the energy to worry about that. Probably because of the thirst. "Let's just hope it rains."

"It will be pouring soon," he says with reassurance. "Let's get inside the plane, it's almost dark. It's dangerous to be outside in the dark."

"Beasts?" I ask.

"And mosquitos. They're more dangerous than beasts."

We each use an insect repellent wipe from the survival kit. Then Tristan grabs the contents of the survival kit he laid out, as well as the mirror shards, and we proceed to the airstairs. Even with Tristan's help, I climb very slowly. He helps me to my seat and shuts the door of the plane. We each eat a sandwich and share the last two cans of soda, which do nothing to still my thirst.

Afterward I lie on the seat I slept on last night. I didn't bother putting it upright this morning or removing the pillow and blanket Tristan gave me last night, so it's already resembling a bed.

"I'm going to the cockpit," Tristan announces.

"Why?"

"To sleep."

"You can sleep on one of the other seats. It'll be much more comfortable than—"

"No, I prefer it that way."

I shrug. "Fine."

I curl up in my makeshift bed, dreading the night. I've suffered from insomnia since I was little. No matter how many sleeping exercises I've tried, I don't sleep more than four or five hours a night. I shiver, my sweat-soaked clothes clinging to me. I have a suitcase with clothes nearby but no energy to get up and find it.

That's when I remember my wedding dress. As if jolted by an electric current, I rise from my seat, looking around for it. It can't be in plain sight, or I would have seen it when I searched for objects to hold water. I sink to my knees, putting my palms forward for support. The light in the plane comes from the moon outside, but it doesn't take me long to spot the creamy fabric of the dress's protective bag under the seat across from mine. I don't open the bag; I can't look at the dress right now. Instead, I go back to my seat, clutching the bag in my arms, and begin to cry. I am glad Tristan went to the cockpit. This moment is mine and Chris's, who must be feeling the same desperation that is rotting me from the inside out.

He'll come for me and Tristan. I know he will.

Chapter 4

Aimee

I wake up still clutching the protective bag in the morning. It sticks to my sweaty, clammy skin, making me wish I could shower. My throat is dry and I look out the window, holding my breath. It hasn't rained. I stumble out of my seat, desperate to get out of the plane. The door is shut, though, which means Tristan is still sleeping. I decide to let him sleep, because he exerted himself more than I did yesterday. I try to open the door myself. I've seen Kyra do it a few times, but since I wasn't paying too much attention to what she was doing, all I manage to do is make a lot of noise as I try to pull it open.

"Whoa, you don't have to disassemble the plane," Tristan's voice booms.

"Sorry, I didn't mean to wake you up."

"Doesn't matter." He comes to the door and effortlessly opens it, turning it into the airstairs.

"It hasn't rained," I say.

"I know."

I descend the airstairs, and walk straight to the fire pit. The fire is extinguished, of course. My heart thrums as my eyes shoot toward the canopy. Anguish swivels inside me, threatening to tear me. Tristan said the forty-eight hours after a crash is when the search is most intense. How many hours do we have left? I make a quick mental calculation. Less than twenty-four.

"It has to rain soon; it's the rainy season. In any case, there are fruits here that contain enough water to keep us going until it rains, but I didn't find any that looked familiar yesterday," Tristan says.

"What are the odds of stumbling upon something that's poisonous?" I ask, my dry throat pushing the thought of any danger besides dehydration out of my mind.

"Let's not find out. We'll walk in a different direction than we did yesterday, look for fruit, and gather some wood in the process."

"Sounds like a plan."

This time when we venture among the trees, I keep my eyes open for fruit that looks familiar. None does, but I'm fascinated by what I see. Plants with thorns so thick they resemble fangs. Fruits that have the texture of berries but are as big as pineapples. Flowers with petals so meaty they must contain water. But the petals are shiny, as if they've been polished with wax, and I remember reading once that it's best to steer clear of shiny things— they may contain poison. As time passes and we walk farther from the plane, things get worse. Every move to cut or pick up branches tires me beyond measure, and my vision blurs. Thirst and hunger erode my concentration and energy with lightning speed. When my legs become too unsteady to be dependable, I stash all the branches I've collected under one arm and grab Tristan's hand with the other one. Since he seems to be stumbling too, I'm not sure if this is a good idea. We're going downhill again, and I wonder how long it'll be until we reach the bottom and what we'll find there.

"Tristan," I say, "if no plane comes... how long will it take us to reach a city if we venture out on foot?"

"Months. We're very deep in the forest. And we'd have to build some sort of shelter every night, which would slow us down."

"Could we make it?"

"It's not impossible, but it would be very dangerous. At any rate, it's not an option right now."

My hands go cold, a spark of fear spreading ice through my nerves. "Why?"

He inhales sharply. "You'll see."

My brow furrows in confusion, as I follow him downhill. A few minutes later, I'm certain we walked into a nightmare. When we reach the bottom of the hill—or at least what I suppose is the bottom—we come at an abrupt halt, unable to move forward. All around us, stretching as far as I can see, is nothing but water. Muddy, dirty water. Everywhere. It must be at least waist-high.

"Is the entire forest under water?" I ask with a shaky voice.

"I suppose there are parts that are not, but most are during the rainy season. It'll be four months until the dry season arrives and the water retreats. Until then, we can't afford to leave this hill."

Four months. If no one arrives within the next

twenty-four hours, we'll be stuck here for four months. And then another thought strikes me. Grim and dark. "Tristan, even if a plane finds us ... where will it land? If there's water everywhere..." Every wisp of air leaves my lungs. "Our hill is covered with trees. How can a plane land without getting wrecked like ours?"

He doesn't answer right away, and his silence sluices away my last tendrils of hope of being rescued.

"They'll use a helicopter. Let's go uphill again," Tristan says. "We absolutely *need* to find some fruit."

Going uphill takes twice as much energy as going downhill did. I take deep, ragged breaths, dragging my feet. I've almost decided to ask Tristan to call it quits and just go to the plane to light the fire when he stops so abruptly I nearly smash into him.

"I think that's a grapefruit tree," he says.

"Are you sure?" I ask. The fruits do resemble grapefruits, except they're much bigger and the peel looks coarser.

"No. But the monkeys are eating it, which means it might be safe for us, too."

"Monkeys?" I tilt my head back and crack a smile. High above us is a group of monkeys.

"Come on, let's take a few of whatever these are and return."

Since the fruits hang higher up, and both of us are too exhausted to climb, we just take the few that have fallen on the forest floor and pile them on the branches we are carrying. By the time we're back to the plane, I can barely stand. Both Tristan and I drop the branches next to the extinguished fire. Tristan proceeds to cut a slice from one of the fruits. Juice drops out of the fruit and I hold out my hand.

"Not so fast," Tristan says, touching the fruit to his lips, holding it there.

"What are you doing?"

"The universal edibility test."

I stare at him, pretending it's not the first time I've heard of it. "We've just established that the monkeys are eating it. That means so can we."

He shakes his head, still holding the slice to his lips. "Not necessarily."

"How long do you do that?"

"Three minutes. Then I'll keep it in my mouth and chew it for fifteen minutes. If nothing bad happens, I'll swallow it, and if I have no adverse reactions to it after eight hours, we can eat it."

"Eight hours? Tristan, are you serious?"

His stiff stance leaves no doubt that he is.

"I'd rather we don't die from poisoning."

I sigh. "You're right. Can you give me a slice to test, too?"

"What's the point of you putting yourself in danger as well?"

His protectiveness takes me by surprise, filling me with a strange warmth. "It's not going to make the process faster anyway," he continues.

"Fine. But the next time we're testing something, I'll do it."

Tristan gives a noncommittal shrug. We build the signal fire, which like yesterday, sends heavy puffs of smoke upward but produces a weak flame, and then build more makeshift leaf baskets to collect water. I have to say, I'm not half bad at this. I manage to weave them much tighter than yesterday. They will hold water for sure. My baskets are far better than Tristan's, which makes me feel less helpless. But not less thirsty. Or less weak.

"You feeling all right?" Tristan asks when I sway. He helps me to the airstairs, and I sit on it.

"Any chance I can eat one slice of the fruit?"

"No, just five hours have passed. We still have to wait three more."

"But—"

"Aimee, I know this is hard, but the human body can go for days without water, though it might feel like you can't go for another minute. Be patient. It's not worth the risk."

I don't argue further, just lean back on the airstairs. After a while I crawl up a step to make a place for Tristan to sit.

"Let's go inside the plane," he says. I crawl up two more steps then can't make it any farther.

"I need a moment to rest."

My humid clothing is almost unbearable. If I move just a few more steps up and go inside the plane, things will be better. Not by much, because it's hot in the plane too, and the air is sticky. But I can't move. And part of me doesn't want to. From here, I have the best view of the sky, and I can also hear a plane or a helicopter, should it come. I press my palms on my eyes, unwilling to let any tears come. I can't lose hope yet.

We should have a heard a helicopter by now. Shouldn't the rescue mission be at its most intense right now? What happens if they don't find us in the forty-eight hour timeframe? Tristan must know, but I'm too afraid to ask him. So I just tune in my ears. Even a faint sound indicating that our rescuers are far off, would be enough for me. But only the ominous sounds of the forest reach my ears. No sound of hope.

My moment of rest turns into minutes, and then hours. I wipe the sweat that clings to my face, the unforgiving reminder that my body is losing water at an abnormal speed.

I doze off.

I wake up with a shriek. Tristan is shrieking, too. No, wait, he's laughing. He's on his feet, his clothing now truly soaked. No wonder—it's raining in torrents.

When I become aware of it, I scramble from the airstairs, landing straight in the mud. I hold my arms up and open my mouth, relishing the touch of the drops that fall with a vengeance. The rain washes the sweat away. A bit of the thirst too.

Tristan and I each drink from the filled cans. After the rain fills them again, Tristan says, "Let's go inside; this would be a bad time to get pneumonia."

Luckily we had the good sense to cover the wood we gathered and didn't use for the fire with those racket-sized leaves, or it would have been soaked by now. We each grab two cans of water and skid inside.

Chapter 5

Aimee

Tristan barely gets the door of the plane closed before we empty the cans again.

"I have a towel in my luggage." I say, grateful I decided to stuff my favorite incredibly smooth, cotton towel in my bag—silly, because I knew there would be plenty of towels at the ranch and at our honeymoon resort. I'm grinning like an idiot, feeling so exuberant I may burst with relief and joy.

"I'll get your bag," Tristan heads to the back of the plane at once, "and mine too. It's as good a time as any to go through our stuff and see what we can do with what we have." We're lucky. Our bags are in a compartment just a few inches away in front of where the trees fell on the plane.

We both have small bags. Tristan has a cabin bag, and mine is just a bit larger. Everything I needed for our honeymoon was already at the ranch. What I have in this bag are a few dresses I packed on a whim, deciding they were better for our fancy dinners at the resort during the honeymoon than the dresses I had at the ranch. Runway dresses made from expensive fabrics and shoes to match—all worthless here, which is why I haven't bothered to unpack.

"I'll go in the cockpit and let you change," Tristan says.

I dry myself with the towel then bend over my bag, trying to decide which dress would be less inappropriate. I pick up a red silk dress and notice a pair of black jeans. I rejoice. I'd forgotten I packed those. I also find two T-shirts beneath the jeans. Well, at least it's something. I slip on the jeans and one of the T-shirts and take the towel to Tristan.

When he comes out of the cockpit he's wearing clothing almost identical to the soaked uniform he discarded: dark pants and a white shirt.

"Should we go through our bags and see what we can add to our supplies now?" he asks. I nod, but there's a knot in my throat as I sit on the floor, staring at my bag. Tristan sits opposite me. My eyes sting a bit and fill with tears as I go through my stuff. I was supposed to be at the ranch or on my honeymoon when I did this. A tear escapes and I brush it away, not wanting Tristan to see me cry. But one glance shows me he's not looking at me at all. He's hunched over his bag, concentrating on something—whether to give me privacy, or because he's genuinely interested in it, I can't tell. But as I go through my things—the white chiffon dress with a navy waistband, the shoes, I almost feel like I *am* on my honeymoon, preparing to start the first day of my married life. I smile.

"I was planning to wear this at our first dinner

in the honeymoon resort," I say, holding up the white dress, smiling. Tristan watches me with an unreadable expression. "And this one on our second night."

"There is still time for them to find us, Aimee."

"Do you really believe that?" I whisper.

He doesn't answer.

"I had each day of our honeymoon planned."

"I have to admit this is something that has always fascinated me about you. You're obsessed with planning everything."

Well, Tristan would know everything about my borderline maniacal habit of planning things down to the most insignificant detail. Long before I had being a bride for an excuse, he had the... privilege... of witnessing my behavior as he drove me around.

"It's a habit I've refined over the years, and it's been very useful. I finished my law degree one year sooner than everyone else," I say, bursting with pride.

"I heard," he says. "You had your whole future planned."

"You didn't?"

He gives a laugh that chills me. "Why waste my energy? You do all that planning and then something like this happens."

"Because crashing in the Amazon rainforest happens every day, right?" I raise an eyebrow.

Tristan snaps his head up, his jaw tight. "No, it doesn't. Let's just drop this."

We make an inventory of the things that qualify as supplies in silence. We have two tubes of toothpaste, two shower gels, two deodorants, two shampoos, and a conditioner. That should be more than enough until they rescue us, Tristan and I agree, though I think Tristan says it for my sake, not because he believes we'll be rescued. I also find a small makeup bag in my luggage, but I put it right at the bottom, because this is the very last thing I'll need here. Tristan brings three magazines he'd forgotten he bought for me when he bought the sodas and sandwiches for the journey. Our phones and my tablet are already dead. There are a total of two blankets and half a dozen pillows in the plane. Then there are the things from the survival kit we inspected yesterday. We also check our first aid kit. Unfortunately, it was at the back of the plane next to the part of the survival kit that was obliterated. Thankfully, only half of the first aid kit was caught under the trunk, so we can still pick out a few items that weren't destroyed: bandages, pads, tweezers, cream to treat insect stings, aspirin, a suture kit, and surprisingly, an unscathed bottle of rubbing alcohol.

I hope we won't need any of it.

I sigh. When Chris's father was doing the travelling, he had a different kind of jet: one of those ultra-luxurious ones with twelve seats and a huge leather couch. He also kept a suitcase with clothes and toiletries permanently on the plane, in case he had to extend his trip somewhere. The plane was always stocked with more food and drinks than were necessary.

When Chris took the company over, he changed to a smaller, six-seat private jet, and always stocked it with just the supplies needed for the journey. While his father loved to indulge in luxury, Chris lived with efficiency. He didn't like showing off or overspending. That was one of the reasons he managed to increase his father's wealth so quickly. He hated waste. I love that about him, but now I wish we were in his father's luxurious jet. It would make a few things easier.

As it is, between Chris's efficiency and the fact that the plane was emptied of all supplies before the inspection, we don't have much. There isn't even one bottle of liquor on board. Tristan knows I don't drink while flying—it makes me sick—so he didn't buy anything. We could use it for disinfection purposes if the small bottle of rubbing alcohol runs out. I shudder. That's no way to think. We won't need another bottle. Heck, I hope we won't even need this small bottle. We'll be rescued in no time.

When the rain stops, we go outside, and are delighted to discover we've collected a decent amount of water. The baskets I made out of leaves yesterday have pulled apart, but the ones I made today hold water perfectly. I want to drink water at once, but Tristan stops me, insisting that we boil it first. I argue that rainwater should be pure, but he says there's a good chance there were microorganisms on the leaves I used to make the baskets. I finally agree, though my throat aches with thirst. I also ask why we couldn't just boil the muddy water from the bottom of the hill and drink it before, but he says he doesn't trust the muddy water not to make us sick, even boiled.

We build a fire with the wood we sheltered under leaves, and boil the water using the empty soda cans as containers. Since we have just four cans, it takes forever to sterilize enough water to still our thirst. Tristan also proclaims the huge grapefruits we gathered safe to eat, so we feast on those. After we're done, Tristan points out that we need to build some kind of shelter where we can keep the wood safe from rain. The large leaves we covered the wood with protected it, but we need something more substantial.

We find what looks like gigantic bamboo trees nearby and use the slim trunks as pillars for a shelter then cover them with the same thick leaves I used to make the baskets. When we finish, it's almost dark. The shelter will keep things dry, but I suspect that if a heavy storm comes along, it will knock the shelter flat in no time.

My stomach begins to grumble after we're done. "We could've used a few more of those fruits," I say, rubbing my stomach.

"I can go get more."

"No. It's almost dark. You said the forest is more dangerous when it's dark."

Tristan frowns as he looks through the trees, making the hair at the nape of my neck stand on end. Not because he's hesitant or frightened. On the contrary. It frightens me *because* he isn't frightened. Not one bit. People without fear are a danger to themselves. My parents weren't frightened of anything. That's how they got themselves killed.

"Don't go in, Tristan," I urge, gripped by panic. "Please don't."

His eyebrows shoot up. He's puzzled by my reaction, obviously. Realizing my fists are clenched, I hide my hands behind my back.

"I'm not that hungry." A loud stomach grumble follows my statement. "I can wait until tomorrow."

"Okay," Tristan says, scrutinizing me. I breathe relieved.

A bird soars above us. Even though it's almost dark, I recognize it by the bright yellow plumage on top of its head. "Look, that's a yellow-crowned Amazon parrot. I have a friend who's had one for years." The bird descends in circles, until it lands on Tristan's arm. "Hey, it seems to like you. I thought wild birds would avoid humans."

"So did I. Can you look away?"

"What?"

What happens next stuns me. He opens his mouth, no doubt to explain himself, just as the bird opens its wings to take off. Tristan turns to the bird, raising his free hand. I think he's going to caress the bird or stop it from flying away.

Instead, he breaks its neck.

I scream, covering my mouth with both hands, buckling forward, and throwing up. Tristan's saying something but I just signal him not to come close to me. I back off, sitting on the airstairs, refusing to look up.

"Sorry. I meant to warn you," Tristan says. "It's just—"

"That was brutal," I cry.

"We need to eat," Tristan retorts.

"Just give me five minutes."

But it takes me more than five minutes to pull myself together. By the time I get up from the airstairs, the now featherless bird is roasting above the fire, speared with a makeshift skewer Tristan built from a piece of metal salvaged from the wrecked wing. The sight sickens me.

"I'm sorry," Tristan says when I approach the fire.

"It's... you just blindsided me."

"I didn't mean to. It should be cooked in about

an hour."

"No edibility test?" I inquire.

"None needed. We both recognized the bird."

"I won't be able to eat anyway." I pace around until Tristan says it's ready. Hunger gets the better of me, and I force myself to take a few bites, though I feel sick afterward.

"Go inside," Tristan says. "I'll clean up around here."

"Thanks." I glance up at the sky. "Why are search missions carried out intensively just in the first forty-eight hours, Tristan?"

"After forty-eight hours they don't expect to find anyone alive. But it doesn't mean they will stop looking for us, Aimee," he says. "Tomorrow morning we'll light the signal fire again. We'll be fine. They'll find us." His tone appears firm and steady, but I detect a tinge of uneasiness under the layers of his reassurance. He doesn't believe they will find us. Fear bites into me hard, but I will myself to remain calm like Tristan. His calmness and fearlessness awe me. And I'm convinced he's not faking. As I watch his well-built frame and heavily muscled arms move in the shadows, I can partly understand why he's not afraid. If I were that strong, I'd feel more courageous... or not. Who am I kidding, I've always been a coward. Still, watching him, I fear a little less.

Lying on my reclined seat inside, I hug the pillow under my head and try to decide which sleep-inducing technique to use. Since I only sleep four or five hours a night, I rely on these techniques to be able to fall asleep; otherwise it can take up to hours for that to happen. But tonight, none of the techniques help. I fall asleep long after Tristan has gone into the cockpit, and when I do, I dream of a helicopter rescuing us in the morning.

Chapter 6

Tristan

No rescue helicopter arrives. Not the following morning, or any morning after it. I expect Aimee to break down, but she doesn't. It shouldn't surprise me, though. I've suspected she is strong since I first met her.

Chris Moore hired me as his pilot two and a half years ago, giving me the chance for a fresh start I so desperately needed. I was grateful to him, and even liked him. Despite his wealth and success, he was grounded and unpretentious. When I first met Aimee, I was pleasantly surprised to learn that she was just as unassuming.

And so much more.

She went out of her way to be friendly, making it easy to adjust to my side job as her driver when Chris didn't need me as a pilot. I suppose I came off as cold to her, because I only acknowledged her effort with a curt *thank you*. But I wasn't used to anyone being friendly to me. Over the past years people had either shown me pity or feared me. Not Aimee. Of course, she didn't know anything about my past—Chris kept his word and never told her.

When first I drove Aimee to Chris's parents' mansion, I realized Aimee hadn't given me any special treatment. She was genuinely friendly to everyone on the staff. They all liked to be around her.

So did I.

I liked it a little too much.

She had a way of growing on people without even trying. She was warm and eager to get to really know people. A bit too eager... and the secrets I carried were best left buried. So I was content with being around her, or observing her from a distance.

From where it was safe.

Here, where our lifeline depends on working and sticking together, where I'm prepared to do just about anything to keep her safe, it will be hard to keep that distance, but I will do my best.

Chapter 7

Aimee

We fall into a good routine in the weeks following the crash. One of the first things Tristan teaches me is how to start a fire without a lighter, insisting we keep the lighter for emergencies. I don't ask what those cases might be. I catch on quickly and soon enough, I can start a fire from scratch without problems, so I take on that task and make sure I build a signal fire every day. Mostly because it keeps me occupied, because I soon lose hope that it will attract rescuers. If Tristan shares my opinion, he doesn't voice it, nor does he make any attempt to stop me.

During our first week, our top priority is searching for familiar plants and fruit. We stumble upon a tree Tristan recognizes: the andiroba tree—the Brazilian mahogany. Tristan claims it's used to treat insect and spider bites. I vaguely recall standing in a pharmacy smelling like a bouquet of freesias in Manaus with Chris and looking at anti-insect creams. Some of them had the andiroba tree drawn on them. The other thing I know about the tree is that most of the furniture in Chris's ranch is made out of it. Since no parts of the tree are digestible, as far as we know, we don't inspect it further.

We don't find any other familiar plants or fruit, so we resort to trying out new ones. I become an excellent monkey spy. At first I watch them from below, then I gather the courage to climb higher in the trees and watch them from there. That's how I discover that high up the trees all sorts of wonders await. Edible wonders. Like eggs and fruit. After my discovery, I start searching for eggs every day, though I don't manage to walk very long distances. The tendrils of heat and humidity pirouetting in the dense air have an exhausting effect on me. We start gorging on the colorful assembly of fruits the monkeys eat. Tristan insists we perform the edibility test on every single new fruit (I managed to convince him to take turns in testing the food), but I don't complain. That's how we discover one of the fruits is not fit for human consumption, despite the monkeys eating it by the bucketful. I was the one testing it, and I had an upset stomach for two days—an experience made doubly dreadful by the fact that nature is our bathroom. Tristan's testing everything himself now. Thanks to his excellent knife skill, we have a meat meal almost every other day. We use the shell of a fruit as a container to boil the eggs. The shell is as hard as stone, and relatively fireproof. Tristan made more skewers from salvaged wreckage to roast the meat.

I knew Tristan wasn't much of a talker, but since it's just the two of us here, I thought he might open up a bit, that he would need to talk. I know I do. But Tristan meets all my attempts at making conversation with monosyllabic answers. He's more talkative when he explains how to do a particular task. So I do most of the talking. I talk about home a lot, but mostly about the wedding.

"I think I may have crossed the line with having twelve bridesmaids," I tell him one day, while we roast a bird. "But every time I tried to take one of the girls off the list, I felt incredibly guilty." Tristan frowns, a sign that bridesmaid talk isn't really something he wants to listen to. So I talk about the music. The cake. At some point I realize *all* the wedding talk makes him uncomfortable. I guess I should have expected it... this is a beloved topic with women, not really a winner with men. Chris himself phased out whenever I talked more than half an hour straight about the wedding. So I resort to talking about home.

"I miss the beach," I say on another occasion, while we search for wood. "Sometimes after work I went to the beach and took long walks on my own. The sound of waves was so relaxing." I stop because talking and carrying an armful of wood at the same time is too much effort.

Survival keeps us so busy I have no time during the day to feel sorry about our situation or ponder over how much I fear that we will never be found. But when the dark sets in, things change. We go inside the plane almost the second the sun sets, because the mosquitos are such pests. We use the insect repellent wipes in our survival supplies sparingly. They don't seem very effective anyway. With the diseases mosquitoes can carry, all we can do is hope for the best. And the forest terrifies me at night. The night reeks of danger, and splinters of fear cling to my senses long after I am in the safety of the plane.

We brainstorm for about an hour about what else we can do to improve our situation. Afterward, Tristan goes in the cockpit to sleep.

Though I appreciate having privacy at night, there is an undeniable sense of loss when Tristan leaves me alone. In the short time we've been here, I've gotten used to him being by my side at all times. This whole thing could be unbearable, but Tristan makes it better. His presence is like an anchor. His gaze, which is watchful and something more I can't quite identify, is heart-warmingly reassuring. I hope I bring him some comfort too.

But at night, there is no escaping my thoughts. They grow darker with every day. The fact that there hasn't been any sign of a rescue plane doesn't help. Neither does my inability to sleep for more than five hours. It gives me too much time with my thoughts. Every night of this first week I fall asleep crying, clutching my wedding dress. Thinking of how desperate Chris must be physically hurts.

Chris and I have been best friends since we were toddlers; our parents were very close. He became my lifeline after my parents died. He became my boyfriend a few months before that happened. I remember worrying that it might be a mistake, that our relationship would be short-lived, and we'd lose our friendship too. We had just started college. Chris was handsome, smart, and the heir to his father's business empire. But Chris remained faithful and loving as the years went by. He remained my best friend as well as my boyfriend. Always by my side. Always up for a good laugh or a meaningful conversation. He knew how to listen to me, and entertain me, no matter what—usually by cracking one of his epic jokes. I swear if he'd failed as a businessman, he would've made a fine living as a comedian. That's what I miss most. His infallible methods of making me laugh. Ironically, I don't miss intimacy that much. But Chris and I never had fireworks cracking between us. Our closest friends used to joke that Chris and I seemed more like brother and sister than a couple. I guess that's true, because we knew each other in ways others didn't. I wouldn't have had it any other way.

At the end of the first week, the day the wedding was supposed to take place, I put the dress away, the sight of it too much to bear.

Tristan and I spend our second week trying to make the place habitable. We build a makeshift shower using the bamboo-like trees as framework and covering them with leaves, placing one of the tightly woven baskets with water above. Tristan, who must have been some sort of magic plumber in his former life, adds a hollow branch as a pipe with some sort of mechanism inside that, by pulling a string, lets water comes out. Since it rains regularly and richly, and we've woven so many baskets to collect water, we have plenty to take up to four showers a day. It's the thing that makes the humidity and sweating bearable. We try to be careful and use as little shampoo or shower gel as possible when we shower or wash clothes, but we're burning through our supplies quickly. Aside from frequent showers, personal hygiene is an issue. Tristan shaves with the pocket knife, and when I get my period, I use whatever strip of fabric I can spare, since I don't have one single tampon with me. I wear my hair in a bun all the time, because otherwise the sweat might drive me to do something crazy like cutting all my hair off. We build a table next to where we usually light the fire, and use fallen tree trunks as benches. The place looks like a very rustic camp, if you overlook the wrecked plane.

I don't talk about the wedding anymore. Thinking of Chris and the wedding depresses me, so I try to avoid it, filling the silence with mindless chatter.

I listen intently to a bird chirping somewhere high above us as I help Trist shape a hollow tree into something we can use.

"This sounds like Vivaldi's *Four Seasons*," I say.

Tristan's head snaps up. "What?" he asks, confused.

"The bird. Listen." For a few seconds, he does. Then his lip curves into a smile. "I think you're right. You're an expert on Vivaldi after all." I can tell he's humouring me, and my cheeks fill with warmth. I often listened to Vivaldi while he was driving me around. Too often, it seems.

"You don't like it? Why didn't you say something whenever I asked you to play that CD in the car? I did ask if it bothered you."

"It didn't bother me at all," he says. "And it seemed to make you happy, so why not listen to it? You always had a blissful smile when *Four Seasons* was playing." Then he bites his lip, as if he said something he wasn't supposed to. Before I get the chance to figure out what, he continues, "What do you like about that song in particular?"

"It's invigorating, like pure energy. I always feel full of life after listening to it."

He nods and then we concentrate on the piece of wood again. My eyes fall involuntarily on the engagement ring on my finger. I try very hard not to think about the wedding ring that I should now also wear. Thinking about how my wedding ring would look on me, I notice something on Tristan's ring finger for the first time. A thin line of skin is lighter than the rest, as if he'd been wearing a ring for a long time.

The words are out of my mouth before I have time to get them through my brain filter. "You were married."

Tristan goes rigid. He follows my gaze to his finger and answers in a measured tone, "Yes, a few years ago, before I started working for Chris."

"What happened?"

Still staring at his finger, he says, deception coloring his tone, "She fell out of love with me." The idea that someone hurt him revolts me. He deserves better. A bizarre wish to protect him so no one hurts him again blooms inside me. Of course, here in the rainforest, the challenge is to ensure that nothing, not no one, hurts him.

"And in love with someone else?" When he doesn't answer I ask, "Are you seeing someone back in L.A.?"

"No."

I see a torrent of emotions in his eyes—most prominently the plea to drop the issue.

I drop it, but this talk of falling in love with someone else tugs at a fear that has sprung up inside me since we crashed. I find myself blurting out, "If you feared you might never see the woman you love again, would you try to forget her in someone else's arms?"

Tristan straightens up. "Chris loves you. Loneliness and pain might drive some people to do things they wouldn't otherwise do, but I doubt Chris is one of those people."

"I wouldn't hold it against him, if he did... something," I whisper. His eyes scrutinize me with an intensity they never have before. When I can't hold his gaze anymore, I look down at my hands.

"You wouldn't?" he asks incredulously.

"I can't imagine how much pain he's in if he believes I'm dead. If being with someone else can lessen that pain..." I brush away a tear. "I just don't think I'll ever see him again."

"Sure you do. Why do you keep building that fire everyday if not for hoping someone will see it and rescue us?"

"So I don't go crazy," I admit. "I know no one will come."

"Even if no one comes, as soon as the water subsides, we'll be able to walk away from here."

"That will take months. And who knows if we'll make it out of the forest alive anyway?" I shake my head, trying to forget I ever said that. I am a positive person, but apparently allowing one dark thought in opened the door to all of them, tormenting me. Tristan puts his arms around me comfortingly, and I sink into them, taking in his wonderful strength.

Each night during this second week I try to think of anything but Chris. I forbid myself to cry. The first few days I fail. When I manage to stop crying, I forbid myself to think of him at all. Memories of Chris—of us—don't belong in this alien place. They belong in our splendid apartment in L.A. and our favorite restaurant on the beach. Or in my old apartment and car. But not here. I can't keep the memories safe here. I can't allow myself to miss him. Missing him is debilitating. And I need all my strength to be able to survive.

The third week, my conscious efforts to distract myself from thinking of Chris pay off, and I find myself thinking of him less often. My constant reminder is my beautiful engagement ring, but I can't bring myself to take it off. There is one moment when the thought of Chris is inevitable. In the morning, when I make the signal fire and look up at the sky. Though there has been no sign of a plane, I still hold the dwindling hope that we will be rescued. Since the chance of that happening is near zero, we walk down the hill regularly to check the water level. It's as high as ever. Tristan says it'll be a little over three months before it recedes enough to try to walk back to civilization. We have to survive until then.

It's also in this third week that I insist we build a fence around our plane. Just the idea of having a perimeter—*something*—separating our space from the forest makes me feel better. Tristan doesn't see the point of a fence, since we can't make one strong enough to keep big predators out in case they decide we're interesting, but eventually he gives in, and we start building one from the bamboo-like tree. The process is arduous and tiring. I'm not used to physical work, nor skilled at it.

Tristan becomes a bit more talkative, but his

answers remain mostly monosyllabic. I want to respect his privacy. I really do. Unfortunately, at this point, I am too starved for human interaction that doesn't consist of working together for food procuring or wood gathering not to push him for more. So while building the fence, I make another attempt. "What did you do before working for Chris? Were you an airline pilot?"

Tristan sighs, and I brace myself for a yes or no answer.

"You should concentrate on what you're doing with that knife. You could cut yourself, Aimee."

I wince at the sound of my name.

"Are you all right?" Tristan asks with concern, his eyes darting to the knife in my hand.

"Yeah, perfect. It's just... it's weird, but when you called my name right now, I realized I haven't heard it in the three weeks we've been here." Goes to show just *how* starved for human interaction I am. "It feels good."

"I can do it more often if you like," he says, shrugging.

Tristan and I jump as a sound splinters the air. It sounds like thunder. That is usually a sure sign a storm will follow.

Usually, when that happens the canopy protects us, and even when the sky explodes in thunders, we have enough time to make a run to the plane before the rain soaks us. The first wave of raindrops floats on the leaves in the canopy, only small ribbons of water trickling down to the floor of the forest. But as more water falls, its weight bends the leaves, and everything gets soaked. That's the usual course.

But this time, there is no rain. We listen for a

while—no other thunder sounds.

"I'd like that, you saying my name."

"It's a nice name, by the way. It means *loved* in French, right?"

"Yeah. My mom spent some time in France and loved it. She spelled my name the French way."

"Aimee," Tristan says, in the same accent my mom did. I wince again.

"Yep, you nailed it."

He grins. "I'll call you like that if you stop pestering me to talk."

I grin too. "No deal. We need to talk, or I'll go insane. I'm used to being surrounded by people all day in the office. And talking to them."

"I'm used to being on my own either in the cockpit flying Chris all over the country, or in the driver's seat in the car. I'm used to silence, so I'm good."

I blush, ashamed that I didn't try to talk to him more often when he was driving me. But he always seemed so unapproachable, so preoccupied with his own thoughts.

"Well, you're stuck here with me. Unless you want me to go berserk, which wouldn't be in your best interest, you'd better put some effort into talking to me. I promise you I'm not as boring as you think."

"I don't think you're boring," he says, stunned.

"Excellent. There's no impediment then."

"Except for the fact that lengthy discussions can break your concentration and distract you."

"I'll take my chances."

Tristan shakes his head. "You must be a damn good lawyer."

"What makes you say that?"

"You just don't give up."

"A spot-on assessment of my skills. I was dyslexic as a kid. My therapist told me I should get a job that didn't require much reading or writing, because I'd have a hard time keeping up." Tristan's eyes widen. "But I always wanted to be a lawyer, like my mom. So I worked hard and became one."

"That's impressive."

"Thanks. It helps that I only need about four hours sleep at night. Lots of time to practice the exercises my therapist gave me. Your turn."

"My turn to what?" he asks a little too innocently.

I scowl, elbowing him. "Where did you grow up?"

"Washington." There it is, the predicted one-word answer.

"Do you have brothers, sisters... did you have a dog growing up?"

He throws his hands up; I've defeated him. I smile and so does he. I finally broke the ice wall—or whatever that was between us. I find out he doesn't have brothers and sisters, and he had two dogs growing up. His parents moved to Florida after they retired, and he visits them a few times a year. From that moment on, whenever we're doing a task that doesn't leave us out of breath, I start a new round of questions. To my surprise, he answers every time, unless I ask about his private life or employment before he started working for Chris. I learn fast to steer clear of those topics and rejoice at every little piece of information he reveals about himself, no matter how unimportant.

Discovering more becomes a sort of guilty

pleasure. The process of gradually discovering things about someone is fascinating. I've known most of my friends forever. I went to college in L.A, where I grew up, so college wasn't much of a discovery experience either. Even my relationship with Chris... well, there wasn't much room for discovery. I felt like I'd known everything about him forever, too. There weren't many surprises or secrets between us. I'd secretly been jealous hearing my friends talk about a first date or the beginning of a relationship, as they learned more about their partner. Of course, when said partner turned out to have a second girlfriend, or was a drug dealer instead of a vet, I'd been grateful there was no unchartered territory between Chris and me. Still, I can't deny the thrill of discovery. Now I have the privilege of experiencing it in snippets the size of teardrops every day.

Chapter 8

Aimee

I wipe my forehead as I scrub one of my two T-shirts on one of the washboards Tristan made two weeks ago. Next to me, Tristan's doing the same with his shirt. We're sitting on one of the massive, fallen tree trunks we use as a bench, each with a washboard between our legs. We've been here a little over a month, and I swear washing clothes is one of the best workouts there is. I glance at my pile of clothing—underwear, two dresses, one pair of jeans and one T-shirt—waiting for me to wash them and curse. I've started wearing some of my dresses, impractical as they may be, because the thin fabric works well in this humid heat. Now I'm wearing a long, red dress with short, wavy sleeves. There's still one dress, aside from my wedding dress, that I didn't touch. The white chiffon dress with navy lace. It's just too long and impractical to wear. It's at the bottom of my suitcase along with other useless things such as my makeup bag.

Tristan pours a few drops of shower gel over my board and then over his. It's not enough to clean the clothes, but it makes them smell better. That's as high as we can hope given our circumstances, and we're very careful to waste as little shower gel as possible.

"What's your favorite color?" Tristan asks. At last he's enjoying our little questioning game and initiates it almost as often as I do.

"White."

"That's a non-color," Tristan says with a smile, tsk-tsking.

"Well, it's the one I like most," I say defensively.

"That's why you have so much white clothing?"

"Yeah," I say, surprised he noticed that. I wore white a lot in L.A.

He nods, as if considering something. "You look good in white."

I blush slightly. One of the wavy short sleeves of the dress I'm wearing falls off my shoulder. I raise my hand to put it back in place as Tristan does the same. Our hands meet mid-way, and when our fingers touch, electricity zips through us. It's so intense, I feel a burning sensation in my fingers even after we break contact. The warmth spreads from my fingers, rising to my cheeks, and I blush, confused, even more so when I realize Tristan is avoiding my gaze.

"You look good in everything you wear," he says, "Aimee."

I flinch a bit at the sound of my name. I usually do when he says it. And he says it often, ever since I asked him to. I can't pinpoint how or why, but it sounds different now.

After a few minutes I ask, "What's your favorite meal?"

He doesn't miss a beat. "Omelette."

I snicker. "That doesn't qualify as a meal," I say, seizing the chance to get back at him for mocking my favorite color. "No one dreams about an omelette. That's a last resort food anyone can cook. Pick something else."

"Well, that's what I like. I love an omelette for breakfast. It's a privilege to be able to eat one while sitting in a comfortable chair, reading the newspaper."

That's a bit weird, but I let it go. Every day here must be a privilege for him since we eat eggs almost every morning, though boiled, not an omelette. Maybe it's his guilty pleasure. Like coffee is for me.

I would understand much later that the privilege is not about the eggs at all, but something else entirely.

"I don't know about omelettes, but I like my coffee in the morning."

"I know," he says, smiling even wider. "At 7:00 a.m. sharp. With one spoon of sugar."

"You're perceptive," I say. "What else did you notice about me?"

"You like to change your haircut every six months and—"

"Wow. You'd make a perfect boyfriend," I say, stunned. "Most men don't notice things like that."

His expression hardens, and I bite my lip. Stepping into forbidden territory again.

"I meant it as a compliment," I add, though I have the feeling that won't help.

"I just like to observe... the little things," he says,

clipping out the words. I mull them over for a few seconds in silence.

"Your hands are almost bleeding, Aimee," he says, alarmed. "I'll wash the rest of your things too."

I look at my hands and notice the skin has peeled off. If I continue rubbing clothes on the washboard, they'll be bloody in no time. My eyes dart to Tristan's hands. They are flushed, but in much better shape than mine.

"Thanks," I say. The tension in his posture ebbs away, and I sigh in relief, glad to be out of the forbidden territory. Why is he so sensitive about his personal life? Maybe he'll open up. A week ago I couldn't get him to talk at all, and now he's asking almost as many questions as I am. But he changes when I accidentally step into his forbidden territory with my questions. His eyes widen, while something I never associated with him creeps into his dark, vivid eyes: vulnerability. So much vulnerability that I want nothing more than to hug him and find a way to lead him to a place of safety. I can't stand the torment in his eyes, the tension that suddenly claims him. Tristan grows on me more and more every day, with every kind thing he does to make things bearable for me, and every soothing word he speaks.

As I watch him rub my jeans on the washboard, I wonder why the employee rumor mill in Chris's parents' household, which was a reliable source of news about everyone's private life, never mentioned anything about Tristan's love life... like the fact that he had been married. I suppose he was as tight-lipped there as he has been with me.

I remember him telling me in our second week

here he isn't seeing anyone in L.A., and I wonder why. I can imagine women would knock themselves out trying to get a date with him. He's stunningly good-looking, with a body so well-sculpted he could give most underwear models a run for their money. His face has beautiful features, with black eyes and high cheekbones. Though for all their beauty, his features are peppered with a harshness I can't place. Like tiny shards of glass in the sun—shimmering bright and beautiful, like diamonds, but cutting at the touch. It's not his looks, though, that make him excellent boyfriend material. It's his heart-melting protectiveness that leads him to taste weird-looking, potentially harmful, fruit himself instead of letting me do it; it's his thoughtfulness to do things for me just to put me at ease, from washing stuff to making sure he calls me by my name a couple of times a day because I asked him to. He'll make a woman very happy one day—if we ever get back to civilization. I remember what he told me about his wife, and I can't imagine why anyone would fall out of love with him.

I rub my numb feet and stand up. "I'm going to look for some fruit for dinner."

"We have plenty of grapefruit, and I'll see if I can catch something. Just rest a bit; there's nothing wrong with resting."

"I feel guilty just sitting here and staring at you rubbing the skin off your hands on that thing."

He laughs, a few strands of dark hair falling into his eyes. He pushes them away, and I can tell he's annoyed with his long hair, but I like it. He asked me to help him cut it a few days ago but I declined, afraid I'd poke his eyes out with the knife.

"No need for guilt. You work a lot. I never imagined you'd be able to do so many outdoor things so well." He says the words with. a tinge of incredulity as if he still can't believe it.

I put my hands on my hips, pretending to be offended.

"I bet you thought I was a spoiled, rich girl."

That isn't far off. My family was rich. Not like Chris's parents, but rich enough. My grandparents had been wealthy, and passed their wealth to my parents, trusting they'd continue the family business and multiply the wealth. But my parents dedicated themselves to humanitarian causes. They donated most of their fortune, though they kept enough for us to have a privileged life. We didn't have household employees, like Chris's parents, which is why I was always a bit uncomfortable when I was at their place, where there was someone ready to meet my needs every moment of the day.

"Well, no, I mean I knew you were down-to-earth, but I was expecting you to complain a lot. You adapt well," he says with approval, and I feel childishly proud.

"Thanks. By the time we leave this place, I'll feel more comfortable outside than inside."

Darkness slithers over Tristan's face and he doesn't reply. Sometimes he's so negative. Despite Tristan's ominous predictions that the forest holds dangers at every step, we've managed to survive unscathed for more than a month, except for discomfort from fruit that failed the edibility test. I may have a false sense of security, but I believe we stand a good chance of getting through the months until the water recedes just fine. These weeks are proof of that.

It won't be long before I realize these weeks have been nothing more than the calm before the storm that never ends.

Chapter 9

Aimee

"**T**his was a definite treat," I say a few days later, rubbing my belly. Tristan hasn't managed to catch a bird in two days, so we've feasted mainly on fruits. Tonight we got lucky. After we're done eating, I announce that since we still have about half an hour left before the darkness sets in, I want to inspect our wood supply, to see if we need to gather more wood first thing in the morning. I still make the signal fire every day. Tristan cleans out the carcass of the bird we ate. While I have no problem eating it, I still get nauseous when I see the bare bones. I wish we had some vegetables to go with the meat, but we haven't had much luck finding any we can tolerate.

I lift myself from the ground with an acrobatic sway caused by a wave of nausea. I regain my balance, shaking my head. I've come to expect this, but that doesn't mean I'm used to it. The humid, choking heat strains my body, and I often find it hard to concentrate on what I'm doing. The mud muffles my footfalls as I make my way to the depleting wood shelter. I inspect the remaining branches, assessing whether they'll be good for starting a fire or just maintaining it. Tristan joins me before long.

"These are no good for starting a fire. Tomorrow morning I'll..." I begin to say when I feel something crawl up my arm. For a few seconds I'm petrified. Then I lower my gaze, and my sweat turns to icicles on my body. My arm is covered with spiders. A twinge of relief wedges inside of me, because they aren't very big. My moment of relief lasts one second, as a horrifying pain grips me, starting where the spiders are. I begin to scream, trying frantically to rub them off, but Tristan shouts something, grabbing my arms, stopping me. How can something so little cause so much pain? It's as if they have sharp knives instead of claws.

"Get them off me," I cry hysterically. "Get them off."

In a swing of his arm, he brushes them away. But the pain persists.

"It's important to—" he begins, but the rest of his sentence transforms into a howl. The spiders get him too. But I don't see them anywhere on him.

"Where is the pain coming from?" I ask.

"My back," he pants, gritting his teeth.

I start unbuttoning his shirt, but he shakes his head, and I understand what he means. No time for unbuttoning. I turn him around and rip open his shirt. I can tell he's trying to say something, but his words mingle with grunts of pain, and all I can manage to make out is the word *palm*.

There they are. Two spiders, on his lower back,

right next to his spine. I slap my palm over them as hard as I can, and they fall off. Tristan's grunts don't stop.

"Let's get inside the plane," I say.

Tristan nods and we half-carry, half-drag each other inside the plane. My arm stings like hell, but I am more concerned about Tristan, who keeps stumbling. His stings were very close to his spine. I shiver. There are a lot of nerves in that area.

"There is insect cream in the first aid kit," he says once I lower him in one of the seats.

"I'll get it." I don't have much faith that the cream will help. We also use the insect-repellent wipes every day, and they aren't very useful.

Tristan makes me apply the cream on my arm first. It looks dreadful. There are red, swollen blotches all over, not just in the places where I was stung. I almost throw up when I see Tristan's back. His entire lower back is little skin hills.

"Your stings look much worse." I apply the cream as best as I can. "What were you trying to say when I was trying to get rid of the spiders on your back?"

"I wanted you to brush them away, not hit them with your palm, because their claws break off and remain inside the skin."

"But that's what I did," I say horrified, looking at his deformed back. "How do I get the claws out?"

"You can't. It's okay, I'll just take more time to heal."

"What if the spiders are venomous?"

"You were bitten about six times. You'd be comatose now if they were poisonous spiders."

I bring him a new shirt from his bag and help him put it on. "Can you help me to the cockpit?" Tristan asks, pushing himself up.

"No way. You are sleeping on this seat. I want to keep an eye on you."

"No." His refusal is strong, more of a command. I'm at a loss for words, so I silently help him into the cockpit. I'm appalled when I see it. It's the first time I've been in it. The place is tiny, and his pilot seat doesn't recline like the passenger seats.

"Tristan, you can't sleep here. There's no space."

"I'll be fine." He sounds so weak; his words are scaring me instead of reassuring me.

"Tristan, please come to the cabin," I plead. He shakes his head. "Don't be stubborn, I promise you I don't snore."

He chuckles, but then his chuckle turn into a grimace of pain. "Close the door and make sure you get some sleep."

Panic wracks me at the thought that something may happen to him. It's so powerful and frightening, it chokes me up, making me forget about my own hurting arm. The idea that something might happen to him is unthinkable. His safety is important to me. Scratch that. *He* is important to me.

I barely get any sleep. My arm bothers me, and I can't stop wondering why Tristan insists on sleeping in that claustrophobic room. I shudder, remembering how weak he looked. Faint sunlight lances through the windows when I finally fall asleep.

Chapter 10

Tristan

The pain persists the entire night, keeping me awake, which isn't necessarily a bad thing. I try to avoid sleep whenever I can anyway. Pain shoots through my back. I grit my teeth and stay still. I've known worse pain. She hasn't, though. I strain my ears, trying to hear beyond the silence surrounding me in the cockpit, beyond the door. The thought that she might be hurting is excruciating. Someone like her should never, ever, know pain. I listen intently to hear if she's crying. She isn't, though she must be in pain—or at least very uncomfortable—from her bites. I breathe with relief. She's stronger than I thought. Extreme conditions tend to bring out the worst in people. But not her, though she looks so fragile.

Of course, one of the first things I found out about her from Maggie, the Moore's elderly housekeeper, was that Aimee wasn't as fragile as she looked. Since I drove Aimee to the mansion regularly, and waited for her for hours, Maggie had plenty of time to tell me stories.

Maggie had been Chris and Aimee's babysitter from the time they were toddlers. She knew Aimee well, and told me Aimee had been through a rough period, losing her parents before starting college. She was proud that Aimee had coped so well—that she hadn't turned into a recluse, and remained kind and warm. That described Aimee perfectly. The first Christmas I spent in Chris's employment, I learned that Aimee buys Christmas presents for every member of the staff. Maggie had told me Aimee had asked around for advice on what to get me, because I was new. But no one could help, since I wasn't close to anyone.

She bought me a picture frame. She seemed uncertain when she gave it to me, but I thanked her politely, in awe that she'd gone to any trouble for me. She bought me a picture frame the second year, too—still looking unsure when she handed it to me, but I didn't have the heart to tell her I had nothing to fill the frames with. The memories I had collected over my adult years didn't make for good pictures. On that first Christmas I started thinking that if I wasn't so beyond hope, if I could have a woman, I wanted her to be like Aimee. Strong. Kind. And why not admit it—I'm no hypocrite—beautiful. I wished Aimee could be mine.

Since we've been here, that wish has grown exponentially. I wish I could take care of her and make her happy in the way she deserves. I wish I could start fresh with her. Together, we'd build enough beautiful memories to fill those frames she gave me. My attempts to keep my distance have grown pathetically weak, because letting her inside my head has turned into therapy. Every little thing I share with her suddenly seems to get a new, brighter meaning. Therapy isn't the right word. Addiction is. A dangerous one, because there are things I never want her to know...

I punch the seat when the pain in my back reaches a level beyond just gritting my teeth. Good timing. The pain rips me from my thoughts. Thoughts I should never have.

Wanting another man's wife should be punishable by law.

Almost wife, I remind myself. Almost. That doesn't make it less unforgivable.

Chapter 11

Aimee

When I wake up the blotches on my arm are almost gone, but I can't move my fingers—my hand, actually. I hurry to the cockpit and find Tristan is already awake. He's so weak he can't stand up. He eyes my arm and my stiff hand, and when I tell him I can't move it he replies, "It'll pass; I'm sure the spiders weren't the poisonous kind. At least not the *very* poisonous kind."

I put up a brave face and help him stand up. He's far worse than I am. He can barely walk, and as soon as we descend the airstairs, he asks to rest. He has a shirt on and won't let me look at his back, instead asking me to bring him a bunch of sticks, the kind we used for the fence and shower. I drop a pile of sticks next to him, and he starts chopping one with his pocketknife, frowning in concentration. He doesn't offer an explanation for what he's doing, and I don't ask for one. Since he can't move, he needs something to occupy his time. I put a can of water next to him.

Considering the position of the sun, it must be past noon. "I'll search for eggs and wood for the signal fire," I say.

He nods, but doesn't say anything.

"Are you in pain?"

"No. It hurt last night, now it's numb. It's like the nerves are paralyzed or something and I can't move by myself." All of a sudden he clutches his left shoulder, grimacing.

"What's wrong?" I ask in alarm.

"Just a cramp," he replies, breathing frantically, one hand groping his shoulder. Without thinking, I put my non-numb hand beside his on his shoulder, squeezing gently, hoping the cramp will pass. After a few seconds it does, and his breathing becomes even, but I continue the light massage, in case the cramp comes back. I'm too preoccupied with my own thoughts to realize his breathing pattern has changed again—it's quicker, sharper. Not because the cramp is back. When something that resembles a moan too much reverberates inside his chest, I freeze. I pull back my arm so fast, my own shoulder snaps lightly. Avoiding Tristan's eyes, I say, "I'll go now."

I'm thoroughly confused making my way through the forest, unsure what to make of what just happened.

A bird in a tree steals my attention. I stare at the tree even after the bird is out of sight. I'm jealous of the trees rising high, high above us. It's as if they want to scrape the sky, steal bits of clouds and sun rays, hide them in their thick foliage, and then drop them in undulating cascades over us, bringing light to the dark beneath the canopy. Some forms of life thrive without light: like moss and ferns. But others don't, and they desperately try to reach the canopy and the light beyond. There are trees that latch themselves onto other trees, enveloping them, strangling them in their fight to find light and escape the suffocating darkness. I empathize with them, though it's not just the darkness that suffocates me. It's the routine of every day, the repetitive tasks required for survival. They threaten to drive me crazy. I yearn to sit in an armchair and devour a good book, or a newspaper. The three magazines in the plane have been read cover to cover multiple times. I've memorized every word. I've read everything, from the technical books of the plane to random instructions written on doors, until I ran out of new things to read. At this point I would be glad to read anything new, even instructions on how to use toilet paper. Anything to break off the repetitiveness would be welcome.

The day passes in a blur. I'm exhausted and move slowly. After finding enough wood for the daily signal fire, I search for eggs. It takes twice as long to find anything, since most of the nests are in the higher trees, and I can't climb high today with my numb hand. It takes a while to find a nest and it only has two eggs in it. That will have to do. Trudging back to the plane, my stomach growls and the sun is starting to set. I build the signal fire first, then cook the eggs. The numbness in my hand is almost gone. When I approach Tristan my jaw drops. He wasn't playing with the bamboo sticks. He made weapons. A few spears, arrows, and two bows.

"I should have made these a while ago, but there was so much to do, I never had the time. Making a good bow takes a lot of time, but these are solid. It should be easier to get food now."

"You need exceptionally good aim to hit anything with a bow and arrow," I say, raising an eyebrow.

"I've got good aim," he says. "It's your aim we'll be working on."

"Why?" I ask, stuffing half a boiled egg in my mouth. I realize just how hungry I am with only half an egg left. At least it's already dark, so we'll go to sleep soon. Tomorrow I'll be climbing trees for more eggs no matter what shape I'm in.

"You need to be able to defend yourself from animals." Considering the howls we hear at night, I can't argue his point. We haven't encountered any predators yet, but that can change. "And you need to be able to keep yourself fed."

I grin. "You're doing an excellent job at it."

"Yes, but you can't depend on me; maybe you'll be forced to do it yourself at some point. Something could happen to me, and you'd be left on your own. You're good at finding eggs and fruits, but..." His voice trails as he registers the shock on my face. The meaning of his words inching to my brain, the shock spreads through me until half of my body is as numb as my left hand.

"Let me look at your back, Tristan," I say in a trembling voice. He hesitates for a moment, then nods. I raise his shirt and gasp. In the light of the flickering fire, I see the skin on his back is twice as swollen as yesterday, and so red I have to look closely to make sure it's not raw flesh.

I want to gag.

"So it's as bad as it feels, huh?" he asks.

"But how...is this all because the claws are still inside?"

"Partly. It might be an allergic reaction. I'm allergic to bee stings, but no other animals. Then again, I've never gotten bitten by this type of spider before."

"This doesn't look like a regular allergy, Tristan."

"Well, did those spiders look like regular spiders to you?"

"Let's get you inside the plane."

I help him to the seat where I usually sleep, then get the first aid kit. "There's nothing except the insect cream, and that didn't seem to do much."

"No, it didn't," he agrees. His forehead is covered in sweat beads. When I touch it, I realize his skin is fevered. "The andiroba tree we saw some time ago, do you think its leaves would help? I don't even know if they can be used if they're not processed..."

I spring to my feet, as an image flashes before my eyes: the pharmacy smelling like freesias I went into in Manaus with Chris, where I saw the anti-insect and arachnid cream tubes with the andiroba tree drawn on them. "Well, it's our best bet." My stomach clenches, remembering the tree was very far into the forest. Farther than I go during daytime without Tristan by my side. "I'll get it," I say, sounding far braver than I feel.

"But you are afraid to go in the forest at night." It's true. Going out of the plane at night terrifies me. The sounds are loudest and most ominous then. "I'm more afraid you might die. I don't want to be alone here."

Tristan bursts laughing. I cover my mouth with

a hand.

"I'm sorry, that came out horrible. I didn't mean it like that..." I say between my fingers.

"Understandable feelings," he says jokingly. "Not the best place to be alone."

"Can you describe the leaves of the tree? I didn't pay much attention, and don't want to risk coming back with the wrong leaves."

His next words come out so weak, I have to strain to hear him. "Well, they are green and..." He takes a deep breath and starts gasping for air.

"Everything around here is green, Tristan. I need more than that," I say, attempting to joke. But Tristan no longer seems to be able to concentrate. Realizing I won't get more details about the plant, I put on my most reassuring smile.

"I'll get it, I remember now what it looks like. I just need a torch." Not the easiest thing to do. I can't just light a branch; it will burn off. Tristan showed me how to make one. A month has passed since then, but I remember the instructions. I need to wrap fabric around the top of the branch, pour animal fat on it, and then light it up. We have fat stored outside, but I need a piece of fabric first. As if reading my mind, Tristan says between gasps, "Take my shirt and wrap it around a branch. The shirt you ripped apart yesterday."

"No. I'll sew that one back together. We can't afford to waste any single piece of clothing." As the words roll off my lips I realize... there is one piece we can afford to waste. One that will never be anything but impractical to wear out here.

My wedding dress.

With small steps, I head toward the back of the

plane where I put the dress. With trembling hands, I unzip the protection bag and suck in my breath.

Strange.

The sight of my dress doesn't unleash the torrent of emotions I experienced when I put my dress away, weeks ago. But the tumult of despair that wrecked me that day rears its head anew as my fingers curl around the knife.

"Don't, Aimee. I know what that dress means to you."

The weakness in his voice snaps me from my moment of weakness like a lightning bolt. I don't hesitate and drive the knife into the fabric, cutting away a strip.

"I'll be back as soon as I can." I hold the white fabric in my hand. "I'll find the tree, I promise."

It's dark outside when I step out of the plane. Very dark. I stumble in the general direction of the wood shelter. I find a branch to make a decent torch and wrap the fabric around it. The makeshift metal container of animal fat is on the floor of the shelter. Tristan stored the fat of a sloth we found dead last week, saying it would be handy in case we need torches. We were supposed to need torches in emergency cases—this counts as one. I put the metal container on the smouldering signal fire, melting the fat, and dip the fabric in it. Then I put the torch over the fire, and it starts burning.

As the flame grows, my breathing slows down, my heart stops racing. This is good. Light is good. Fire is good. Beasts are afraid of fire, aren't they? Nothing will attack me while I have this. Holding the torch up, I enter the forest, clinging to this idea. I take small steps deeper in, and I feel a dreadful tingle on my feet; something is trying to crawl up my running shoes. The creatures slithering on the forest floor don't care about my torch. Trying not to concentrate on them, I keep my eyes on the flame, watching it burn the white fabric. I once read white is the color of hope, so I chose white instead of ivory for my wedding dress, because I found hope fitting for a wedding. Hope for happiness. A bright future.

How bittersweet to watch that hope burn away shred by shred. I tighten my grip on the branch, hearing howling sounds around me. My heart rate picks up; sweat breaks out on my forehead. What's making the sounds? Some sort of owls? Monkeys? Or something worse? I wish I couldn't hear them, but if there is something inescapable here, it's the sounds. The jungle never sleeps.

It feels like I've walked forever when I reach the place where we saw the andiroba tree. I try to remember what its leaves looked like. Long and oval, perhaps. I spin around, looking for one with oval leaves. I see trees with round leaves, star-shaped leaves, spines, and no leaves at all. But no oval ones. I go in circles until I notice one with leaves that come closer to oval than anything else. I cut a few handfuls of leaves then realize I didn't bring anything to carry them in. Brilliant, Aimee. Just brilliant. I pull at the hem of my T-shirt and put the leaves in it. Keeping my eyes firmly on the leaves, trying not to drop any, I walk back to the plane. I'm halfway to the plane when I hear a growl. Animals are afraid of fire, I remind myself. I'll be all right. But the light from my torch is significantly weaker. I raise my gaze from the leaves to the torch and stumble in my steps.

The flame.

It's almost gone. I remember Tristan telling me such a torch would last ten or fifteen minutes. I've been gone longer than that. My feet shoot forward at the same time panic sets in. I run, faster than I ever have, terrified I will lose the leaves, but more terrified that the flame will vanish, and I won't find my way back. Pain slices my calves from the effort, branches scratch my cheeks, as I move faster. The light goes out before the plane comes into view, but I'm almost there, so I keep running, tripping, falling, rising, and then running again, until I find the entrance in our makeshift fence. I don't stop until I reach the airstairs. I drop the useless torch, grabbing the airstairs to steady myself. I'm shaking like a leaf, fighting hard the urge to collapse. I don't look at the T-shirt I'm clutching, for fear I might have indeed lost all the leaves. When I can't postpone the truth any longer, I look down and breathe with relief. I've lost a lot of the leaves, but there are enough left to hopefully help. I grab one of the water baskets. If his fever doesn't subside, he'll need to keep hydrated.

Tristan is worse. Much worse. He's pale and soaked in sweat. Despite that, he smiles when he sees me. "I was worried something happened to you."

"How did you find any energy to worry about me?" I say, filling our soda can with water and helping him drink. My fingers touch his cheek. He's burning up.

After drinking the entire cup he says, "You're not the only one who isn't overjoyed with the idea of being alone in this place." I flush, remembering my insensitive comment from earlier, dread overwhelming me as he grins again. The fact that he forces humor in his voice means he's not just looking, but also feeling, worse. I show him the leaves. "These are the ones I meant, yeah," he says.

"Let me put them on the stings."

It's all I can do not to vomit as I take off his shirt, apply more of the insect cream, and then cover his back with leaves. I'm not very optimistic, but I try not to show it.

Tristan keeps talking while I sink one of my T-shirts in water and put it on his forehead as a compress. Since the water is not cold, it doesn't help bring the fever down, but it seems to make it more bearable for him. His words come out weaker, until they are almost whispers, and I have to strain my ears to understand him.

"Help me back to the cockpit," he whispers.

"Are you insane? I'm not moving you anywhere. You're staying right here. I'll keep putting water on your forehead."

"No... I"

"Shh. Don't argue. You'll sleep here."

I soak the T-shirt in water and also run it on his arms and chest this time, because his whole body is burning. He insists on returning to the cockpit, but the fever takes the better of him and he falls asleep, with his head in my lap. A terrible thought wedges its way into my mind. What if he won't wake up? What then? I shake my head, trying to dispel the thought. I look around, searching for something else to think about. My calves provide a welcome, if superficial distraction. Since our daily tasks are a constant workout, my body has changed a bit. The fact that our food is very protein-heavy also contributes. My calves and arms are stronger than they used to be, though I can't say I like them. They look bulky. Tristan's body has also undergone similar changes, but the muscles look good on him. They make him look strong, unbeatable. Yet as he lies here with his eyes closed, all his energy stripped away, he looks defeated. His body succumbed so easily to illness. When I see him like this, it's hard to believe he's the same man who ventures in the forest every day with nothing but a knife—who doesn't seem to know fear. Now he's weak. Vulnerable.

It feels weird—almost like an intrusion—having him in the cabin with me. I was used to it being my place. Unfairly so, since the cockpit is so small.

I shift in my seat, dipping the cloth in water, when Tristan starts mumbling. I think he's trying to tell me something at first, but then I realize he's still asleep. His mumbling gets louder, and he begins to twist around, his fingers groping and scratching at the seat. Out of his incoherent gasps, I make out the words *run*, and *I'm sorry*. I try to shake him awake from his nightmare, and when my hand touches his chest his eyes flutter open. They are unfocused, but deep behind their confusion lies something that bewilders me. Terror. Like the gaze of a hunted animal. I want to comfort him somehow, to tell him it's just a nightmare; he's all right and I'll take care of him. I wish I could find a way to make him feel safe, like he does when we're out in the wild. But before I can do anything, he grabs my hand.

"Don't let go," he mumbles, his eyes closed again.

"I won't," I answer, petrified. He relaxes, still

mumbling gibberish. At least he doesn't twist anymore. Every time I try to move my hand to shake the numbness away, spasm wrack him, and his mumbling intensifies, so I try not to take it away. Even though it feels SO numb, I'm afraid it might fall off. Doesn't matter. I'd do anything to ease his despair. Realizing how important his well-being and happiness is to me stuns me. I have never felt so desperately needed, or seen anyone so terrorized by a nightmare.

The fever must be giving him nightmares.

Or is it?

I remember how he wanted me to take him back to the cockpit. How he insisted on sleeping there since we've crashed, even though there's enough space for him to sleep here. How he closed the door to the cockpit every night. Does he go through this every night? Is this why he seeks solitude? Whatever is behind his eyelids frightens him, that's for sure. I shiver.

What can frighten this man who isn't even scared in the rainforest?

Despite getting no more than two hours of sleep, I feel energetic in the morning. Tristan's fever subsides. Doubtful that my compresses were of any help, I check the leaves while he's still sleeping. No idea if they worked, but his back looks far better than yesterday. I put fresh leaves on the stings and let him sleep while I leave the plane and start the daily routine with the signal fire and looking for eggs.

Chapter 12

Tristan

I wake up briefly. At first I think the pain in my back might have woken me, but that's not it. Then I understand what did. Her absence. Before I fall back asleep, I acknowledge that last night, for the first time in years, I found peace in my sleep. I know what brought it. Or rather, who brought it.

My peace carries her smell and sounds like her voice.

It feels like her touch.

But I have to give up that peace.

With a bit of luck, she'll think that last night's nightmares were caused by the fever. Tonight I will return to sleep in the cockpit, though I never wished for anything as intensely as I wish now to be by her side. If I stay, she'll realize the fever isn't at fault for my nightmares.

Before she can give me peace, I will take hers away.

And she will hate me for it.

Chapter 13

Aimee

I boil three of the six eggs I collected and eat them quickly. I wonder if Tristan is still sleeping. I'm about to boil the others for Tristan when I have an idea. I retrieve a flat piece of metal from the wing wreckage and place it over the fire, heating it up. In the meantime I crack the eggs in the fruit shell bowl and stir them with a wooden stick. On a whim, I slice the fruit that resembles grapefruit and add it to the mix, pouring everything on the piece of metal. I end up with a burnt omelette, but an omelette nonetheless.

Tristan is still asleep. I sit on the edge of the seat, holding up the omelette right under his nose. He wakes up with a start.

"What the—" he stops when he sees the omelette. "What's this?"

"Ha, ha. It's an omelette. A burned one, I admit."

His eyes widen as he takes a bite, then smiles.

"You put grapefruit in it?"

I shrug. "Since we're in the rainforest, why not add some local flavor to it?"

"Thanks. This is good. Do you want a bite?"

"I'll stick to boiled eggs. I hate omelettes."

He jerks his head back, smiling. "You prepared this just for me?"

"Thought you deserved to be spoiled a bit after what you went through last night. It is your favorite course after all." I like doing something that puts a smile on his face, seeing him happy. It fills me with relief and something else I can't identify. Surely, if he smiles, he can't be too sick. The panic from the night when we were bitten hits me in a whipping flash, the terrible fear that something could happen to him or that I could lose him wedging inside my mind. I shake the thought out, concentrating on his smile.

"Wow. You remembered that."

"Of course. Why did you think I was asking?"

"To make conversation," he says through a mouthful.

"Do you mean you don't remember anything I've told you?" I ask with fake horror.

Tristan lowers his gaze to the omelette.

"What's my favorite color?"

His blank expression tells me he was indeed just making conversation. I sigh, shaking my head.

"How are you feeling? Your back looked better."

"It's still uncomfortable, but nothing like yesterday."

"Do you think those leaves worked?"

"No idea, but it's possible. The seeds' oil is used in creams, but maybe the leaves are useful too. I feel much better. And I've slept better than I have in a long time."

If his voice didn't have this strained edge to it, I'd guess his comment was coincidental. But I don't believe it is. I steal a glance at him. His fingers clasp the edges of the metal makeshift plate. His features reflect the strain of his voice. He's testing the waters, though I'm not sure what he's testing them for. Does he remember he asked me to stay with him last night and is ashamed? Or perhaps he wants to explain his nightmares. Since he doesn't offer more information, I just say, "I'm happy to hear that."

He steers the conversation in a different direction. "You were very brave yesterday, to go after the leaves," he says, taking another bite.

"I'll go back and get more today, before nightfall. I lost some on the way back, and you might need more leaves."

He frowns. "That's not a great idea. I don't feel well enough to come with you, and I don't want you to venture so far again by yourself."

"But what if you need more?"

"We have enough for today and tomorrow. I might feel better then and come with you."

"Okay..."

He runs a hand through his hair. "I should show you how to handle the weapons."

"That'd be good, yeah." I shudder, remembering the growl last night. If anything had attacked me... well, I'm not sure how helpful a weapon would have been. I had enough trouble just holding the torch and the leaves.

I remember something and burst out laughing, but there's no humor in it.

"Aimee?" Tristan asks, uncertain.

"I was supposed to find out today if my boss had assigned me to one of our biggest cases. And now I'm contemplating learning how to shoot with a bow. A bit ironic."

Tristan lifts himself up from his seat, motioning me to help him out of the plane. I put one of his arms around my shoulders, and we stagger out of the plane.

"You need a shower," I say to him, half-jokingly.

"Trust me, I'm aware. Help me get in the shower. My back still feels like it's paralyzed."

I lead him inside the wood cubicle and wait for him on the airstairs. He takes longer than usual in the shower, but given he can barely move, it's not surprising. I help him when he comes out, holding him up as best as I can.

"Some nerves in my back," he says through gritted teeth, "if I move a certain way, they hurt. Otherwise I just can't feel my back."

I sit him on the airstairs and bring him some water to drink. He drinks with large gulps, the hush of the water pouring down his throat filling me with anxiety.

"Better?" I ask.

"Nope. Distract me."

"Hey, I already cooked an omelette. I've run out of ideas for the day. Scratch that, for the week." I've never been good at this. Distracting and entertaining people has always been Chris's territory.

Tristan frowns, as if he's considering something. "You're a corporate lawyer, right?"

"Yes," I say, swaying from one foot to the other. "Do you want me to talk about my job? It won't distract you. More like bore you to tears."

"No, it's just that... Maggie said you wanted to be a human rights lawyer until you started college."

Ah, the household rumor mill again. It doesn't upset me, though. I could never be upset with Maggie. She's like a second mother to me. I'm glad Chris's parents kept her as their housekeeper after we grew up.

"I changed my mind," I say, my tone clipped.

"How so? It's a big step from human rights lawyers to corporate lawyer."

Though his tone is not in the slightest judging, or accusing, I feel defensive.

"Just because," I snap, but then soften at his stricken expression. "I'm sorry. This is a very sensitive area for me."

"Your career choice?"

I sigh, sitting on the airstairs, one step beneath him. No one asked me why I decided to change my career, though everyone knew I was dreaming of being a human rights lawyer. After my parents' death, it was sort of implied why I changed my mind. Or, well... not why. People never understood why. They just assumed that the traumatic event had something to do with my decision. But that didn't keep people—my closest friends, even Chris—from judging my choice.

"Do you know how my parents died?" I ask.

Tristan inhales. "No."

"Umm..." I pick a spot on the airstairs and gawk at it, fiddling with my hands in my lap. "My parents dedicated their life to charitable causes. This meant more than donations or charity parties. They'd often fly to underprivileged countries to give out food and medicine, and oversee infrastructural projects. They were my heroes when I was little and into my teenage years, even though they were gone for long periods at a time. I rarely saw them." Warmth feathers me on the inside, as I remember checking the mailbox, and later my email, waiting to hear from my heroes—to learn when they'd be home to spend time with me and tell me about their latest achievements.

"Before long, they also got involved in the politics of countries that were... politically unstable. Wherever the danger was greater, there they were, both of them. Wanting to bring hope to places where there was no hope. They were fighters. They believed they could make a difference. The week after I turned eighteen they went to one such country that was on the brink of a revolution. The revolution started a few days after they arrived there, and they were killed." The warmth inside me turns to an engulfing flame—the flame that turned all the memories and thoughts of my parents into a source of misery and anger instead of the happy place they used to be before their deaths. "The world isn't a better place. And they are still dead. What was the point?"

Pain pierces my palms, and I look in my lap, discovering I've dug my nails very deep in my skin.

"The point is, it's people like your parents who help this world become better every day, even if you can't see it right away. They did a lot of good. I read an article about them once. They were good people. Fighters." His voice is gentle, but every word feels like the lash of a whip.

"Oh yes, they were fighters. They fought with

everything they had to bring good to the world. They sacrificed anything for that. They gave everything to the world. And what did the world give them back? Nothing," I spit. I don't dare meet his eyes, for fear I'll find the same accusatory look that Chris had when I spoke like this in front of him. But I can't stop myself from spitting out more words. Wrong words. "The world took everything from them. And it took them away from me. You're right, they were fighters. But I wish they hadn't been, so they'd still be alive. When I was little, I dreamed of my father walking me down the aisle to give me away. Chris's father was going to do it, because my dad isn't here to do it."

"You are bitter." Tristan slides down the steps until he's on the same level. I still avoid looking at him.

"Yes. And selfish. Lamenting that my father isn't here to walk me down the aisle. What a tragedy, right? When there are real tragedies going on around the word. Tragedies they were trying to prevent. I used to want to be a human rights lawyer because I wanted to follow in my parents' footsteps. But after they died, I became a different person. I didn't want anything to do with *anything* they did. So yes... that's how I went to the other extreme and became a corporate lawyer. I bet my soppy story wasn't what you wanted to hear." I try to sound humorous, like the whole thing is a joke.

"There's no shame in what you did, Aimee. It's a natural reaction to want to distance yourself from your parents' world and ideals. You associate that with pain. You don't have to feel ashamed. I'm not judging you, Aimee."

His words—so simple, so serene—have a calming effect on me. Like sprinkling honey on a burn, they rein in the fire that scorches me, soothing the cracks that the contained pain and shame have cut inside me.

He tilts my head until I meet his gaze, as if to make sure I got his point. But neither his words nor his gaze manage to silence the raucous thoughts tormenting me.

"I am not a fighter, like them," I whisper. "If I were, I wouldn't have given up so easily. I'm a selfish person." Tristan opens his mouth, then closes it again without uttering a sound. I pull away from him. "Go ahead, say it. Everyone else had no qualms with letting me know how they feel about it."

"You're not selfish. If you were, you wouldn't have gone for those leaves last night. The forest terrifies you when it's dark."

"That's not tipping the scale in my favor. But then again, compared to all the things my parents did, nothing I do will tip it in my favor."

"I'm sure they would be proud of you anyway."

This has haunted me since my first workday. "No, they wouldn't. Not at all." I rise to my feet, walking to the signal fire, putting more branches on it. My confession to him drained me of energy. But it also drained something else... a rotting negativity I have accumulated over the years. I feel more at peace than I've felt in a long time.

Tristan takes the cue and doesn't pursue the topic. "Ready for some shooting training?"

"I guess."

"We need a target."

Tristan's back cracks when he attempts to stand,

and I push him back on the steps, assuring him I'm capable of doing this on my own. I build a makeshift target by curling a few branches and putting leaves inside them. I get the bows, arrows, and spears from the wood shelter and drop them at Tristan's feet. Then I realize...

"Can you shoot with your back?"

"No. Arching my back hurts. But I'll explain it to you the best I can."

Turns out no matter how much Tristan explains what I have to do, I can't shoot straight to save my life. The arrows don't touch the target, instead flying below, above, or to its sides and into the bushes. The process becomes cumbersome, because I have to retrieve all the arrows. Eventually, Tristan stands up. He does it slowly and doesn't seem in pain—just uncomfortable. He presses his hand on my stomach, explaining that I have to center my weight there.

When his hand touches my stomach his breath catches, and he bites his lip. I pretend not to notice, though my own breathing intensifies with shame, my stomach jolting. I try to concentrate on shooting, but I find myself peering at him often to see if he continues to bite his lip.

He does. His reaction makes me uneasy, and I have no idea what to do about it, but something stirs inside me. With bewildering confusion, I realize what that is: guilt.

No amount of instruction helps. I give up after about three hours, dropping the bow. "I suck. There's no other way to put it."

Tristan, who's once again resting on the airstairs, shakes his head, saying, "You'll get better with practice."

"I'll go cut fresh leaves to replace the ones in the shower. They're decaying already."

I spend an inordinate amount of time cutting the leaves, using the alone time to put my thoughts in order after the events of the last hours. I trudge back, my arms full of leaves, and start patching the shower. Tristan is nowhere in sight, so I assume he managed to drag himself inside the plane to rest. I fiddle with the leaves before I weave them into a curtain. I replace the old curtain, my heart swivelling inside me with ridiculous pride, as if I've just built something very complex.

I jump when I feel a tap on my shoulder.

"Sorry, I didn't—" I stop, seeing Tristan carrying white flowers. "What are these?"

"White flowers. White is your favorite color."

I slit my eyes. "You were pretending not to remember, then."

This wins me a boyish grin from him. "Gardenias are your favorite flowers, and I would've gotten you gardenias, but the rainforest is out of them. Or at least not anywhere near the fence. I couldn't go searching very far because of my back."

"Oh! Your back. You shouldn't have gone—" I don't finish my sentence because Tristan places the flowers in my arms, and his gesture renders me speechless. He remembered my favorite color is white, and he went to search for flowers despite his back. He leans against the shower cabin, massaging his back, breathing hard through gritted teeth.

Such a normal act... receiving flowers. It unsettles me. I try hard not to think about my normal life at home on any day. Most of the time I succeed, when I lose myself in tasks such as fence building or food searching. But this is a drop of normalcy in the vertigo of madness. A reminder that there's more to life than survival. Even here.

In a move that surprises me just as much as it surprises him, I fling my arms around his neck, pulling him into an embrace. "Thank you, Tristan," I whisper.

"I'll slice some of the grapefruit you brought in this morning," he says when we pull apart.

"All right. I'll see if the signal fire needs more wood."

The fire looks just fine, so I end up sitting next to our wood supply, hugging my knees. I hold a thin branch in one hand, absent-mindedly scratching the mud.

"What are you doing?"

I flinch, startled, then rise to my feet. "Wasting time. Sorry."

Tristan frowns, pointing at the mud. "Is that part of a poem?"

"Is it?" I look over the scratches I painted in the mud and see, with surprise, what I thought were scratches are indeed words.

The descending blue; that blue is all in a rush
With richness; the racing lambs too have fair their fling.
What is all this juice and all this joy?

"It's from 'Spring' by Gerard Manley Hopkins. I didn't realize I still knew these lyrics. I haven't read poetry since high school."

"You miss reading, don't you? I saw you already read the magazines."

"Several times. I'd love to read something new. Anything."

He squints his eyes. "I have an idea." Picking up another branch, he starts drawing shapes in the mud. Letters. I drink each one in as soon as he draws it.

You are not wrong, who deem
That my days have been a dream;
Yet if hope has flown away
In a night, or in a day,
In a vision, or in none,
Is it therefore the less gone?

"Do you recognize it?" Tristan asks.

"No. Who wrote it?"

"Edgar Allan Poe. It's from 'A Dream Within a Dream.' I like his work."

"It's kind of a pessimistic poem."

"That's not the point. You said you wanted to read something new, so..."

"Thanks. Do you remember more of the poem?"

Tristan grins. "Right now, I'm too hungry to remember anything other than how to eat this." He glances sideways at the slices of grapefruit.

It takes almost two weeks for Tristan's back to heal completely. During that time he moves carefully, helping me wash clothes, and occasionally bringing me flowers, but unable to do much more. We eat meat once, when a bird lands on Tristan's shoulder. We live off the eggs and fruit I collect, and we both drop weight. After testing a few roots that fail the edibility test, we find an assortment of four carrot-looking roots we can eat. They taste like nothing, but they fill our stomach. He insists I train with the bow, but I'm not making much progress. It doesn't help that he can't show me how to shoot. He does try to show me once, but the simple movement of arching his back must strain some nerves, because it has him stuttering with pain and has him unable to move for the rest of the day. Still, I'm not bad with a spear, and that gives me some confidence.

Tristan sleeps in the cockpit again. Despite feeling his presence in the cabin was an intrusion the night the fever overtook him, the place feels empty without him. Falling asleep becomes harder than before, and I find myself staring at the ceiling for hours at a time. My thoughts don't fly to Chris often, like in the beginning. Perhaps my self-imposed ban on thinking about him is turning into something that comes naturally. Or perhaps my mind knows that the way to make living in this place bearable is not envisioning what the alternative would be: Chris's ability to make me laugh, and a life in which my biggest worry would be losing a case; not starving or succumbing to disease or walking into a nest of vipers—which I almost did. Twice.

And because my mind apparently needs something to obsess over, once I stop obsessing over how my life would be if I weren't stuck here, I start obsessing over something else.

Tristan's nightmares.

I hear him thrashing in his sleep every night, even though he closes the door to the cockpit. I wonder why I never heard him before. I suppose I was too busy with my own thoughts.

Now that I know about the nightmares, I can't help hearing them. They happen every single night. No exceptions. A few times I find myself hovering in front of his door, wondering if I should go in and wake him up, try and soothe him. But I don't. He wouldn't appreciate it; he's adamant to keep to himself. And I'm not sure that would help him at all. But I'd like to try to help him, like he helped me the day we talked about my parents. I carry his words with me all the time—they're like a talisman, those words—they work even when I am not actively thinking of them. From time to time, I revisit my old inner cracks, carved by guilt and loss. I find the cracks are less painful with each visit.

Now, if only I could do something so the cracks carved into him, by whatever happened in his past and causes him nightmares, wouldn't hurt so much. He's become important to me in a profound, almost vital way. Listening to him cry out is unbearable. And if it's unbearable for me, I don't want to know what it feels like for him.

One morning we find paw prints just outside the fence. Huge ones. Tristan says they must belong to a feline of some kind. A cougar, or maybe even a jaguar. After the discovery, we're more alert than ever when we venture outside the fence. One more threat looming over us in the months we still have to wait before we can start our journey back.

Chapter 14

Aimee

"I know this one. It's nice," Tristan says on the day that marks two months since we crashed and almost two weeks since the spiders bit us. His eyes light up as he reads the snippet of the poem I scratched in the mud again. This has become an almost daily thing—like an unspoken agreement. When we sit to eat dinner, or sometimes—like now—breakfast, we write a few lines in the mud.

I don't recognize any of the poems he writes down, which is a bit embarrassing since he quotes authors that anyone who was a top student (which I was) should know. At any rate, it feeds my need for reading new things. It's like a small escape every day. It breaks the repetitiveness of our survival tasks; it's something new to look forward to—something new that doesn't revolve around the act of procuring food.

It's a luxury, and we both indulge in it.

His poems intrigue me. Edgar Allan Poe isn't

the only writer he likes. Thomas Hardy is one of his favorites among many, many others. But no matter which poet he quotes, all the verses have something in common: they speak of pain, darkness, and acts that are beyond forgiving.

I don't understand why he's into this kind of literature. There is beauty in it, sure. It's just a bit depressing. In the beginning I thought it was just his taste, but now I suspect it might be something else.

In our question rounds during chores, he's careful to stay away from unpleasant topics, and I've learned not to push him. But when he scratches words in the mud, things change. His eyes have that same tide of emotion they have when I accidentally slip into topics he doesn't want to discuss. That's why I suspect his refuge in depressing poetry is related to those less joyous experiences he keeps from me. With every poem he shares, that inexplicable urge to hug him—or find a way, any way, to comfort him— grows. I want to make his dark cloud disappear. I need it to disappear, because I can't stand to see him tormented.

I'm learning almost as much about him from the few lines he writes in the mud every day as I do from our questioning when we do chores. I counter with poems that couldn't be more different. They're cheerful and light. It's not that I was ever into cheerful poetry; I was never into poetry at all. I like novels. I'm surprised I remember any poems at all. The last time I read poetry, I was a high school senior. For some reason the sunny, bubbly poems stuck. At any rate, Tristan seems to show as much interest in my poems as I do in his.

When we finish with the poetry session, I hand Tristan the bow and arrow. "This is your chance to impress me." He claims he feels well enough to teach me how to shoot.

He frowns, positions the arrow, and pulls the string of the bow. I try to memorize every action, every movement of his muscles, hoping to be able to reproduce them when my turn comes. His wide shoulders hunch forward, his strong arms gripping the bow and the arrow. The muscles on his arms and shoulder blades are flexed; I can see their sharp contour beneath his shirt. The muscles on his stomach are tightened, too. The defined packs on his abdomen are visible through his damp, clinging shirt. He told me time and again that in order to hit the target it is most important to find my balance and keep myself centered. He claimed I could achieve that if I contract my abdominal muscles. I've tried, but I see now that I haven't done it properly.

Tristan aims at our makeshift target. And misses it by two feet. I start laughing. "I'm not impressed."

I am still laughing when Tristan releases the second arrow, which hits the target right in the middle. As do the third and the fourth. He launches the fifth one up in the air at a bird that passes over us. I yelp, covering my mouth with my hands when the bird lands on the ground, the arrow stuck in its chest. He aims the next arrow at the target again, hitting straight in the center cluster. The same with the arrow after it.

And that's when the pieces of the puzzle start coming together, one arrow at a time. His knowledge of survival skills, like building a fire from scratch and the edibility test. His nightmares.

"You were in the Army," I say.

Tristan's knuckles whiten on the bow, his jaw tightening. He lowers the bow, walking to the target to collect the arrows, and then picks up the fallen bird. Not once does he glance in my direction.

"Tristan?" I ask. "Am I right?"

He slumps on the tree trunk that serves as a bench, and hunches over the arrows, inspecting their tips.

"Yes. I was deployed in Afghanistan." His voice is freakishly calm, almost impassive. I sit next to him, a sudden wave of admiration engulfing me.

"We should find some poison to dip the tips of the arrows in," he blurts out.

His words bewilder me so that I don't have time to ponder whether he's trying to change topics or really plans to poison the arrows. "Why? That would make whatever you shoot with a poisoned arrow inedible, right?"

"Not for the animals we intend to eat, but for predators." I know he's thinking of the paw prints we discovered the other day. "If a jaguar makes an appearance, I'd need about five arrows to take him down. Jaguars are very fast. I'd never have time to shoot enough arrows. If the arrows are poisoned, we'll have a better chance."

"How will we find poison? I mean, most things around us are poisonous, but it's not like we can drain—"

"I don't know yet." He rests his jaw on his palm. The tuft of dark emotions in his gaze tells me he's not thinking about poison for the arrows, but a different kind of poison.

"That's what your nightmares are about, aren't

they?" I ask. "Your time in the Army."

He doesn't answer, but I won't be deterred. "If there's an elephant in the room—or well, the jungle—I don't want to keep ignoring it. We can talk about things. It can be liberating." I remember the talk we had about my parents a few weeks ago, and how I felt so much freer afterward. When Tristan doesn't glance at me, much less answer, I add, "I hear you every night, you know."

That makes his head snap up. "You can hear me?"

"Yeah." His gaze holds so much anxiety and desperation that I'd like nothing better than to bury myself in the ground, ashamed that I'm intruding in a matter so private.

He swallows hard, looking away. "I'm sorry."

I blink, confused. "For what?"

"I didn't want to disturb you. I thought if I closed the door... I didn't realize I was so loud."

"You're not disturbing me. You don't have to keep sleeping in that cockpit. There is enough room in the cabin, and I don't get scared by nightmares."

He smiles sadly. "No, but you will resent me. Even if you can hear me when I'm in the cockpit, it's better if there's a door between us."

"I won't resent you. Tristan, come on, trust me on this one. You need to be able to rest. The cockpit is nowhere as comfortable as the cabin. We'll deal with those nightmares."

He glances at me, his expression unreadable. Then he hands me the bow and some arrows.

When our fingers touch, an electrical current shoots through—just like the day he told me I look good when I wear white. Only now, I realize with a jolt of my stomach, it's even more intense. I've been paying attention to these reactions from him. They happen often lately. They are becoming harder to ignore, but I try my best. Something else is getting harder to ignore, too.

This sense of guilt I can't place.

"Let's get you to shoot straight," Tristan says in a voice that doesn't sound quite right. "I'll deal with my nightmares."

I smile. "Let's make a deal. I let you teach me how to face the forest; you let me help you face your nightmares."

"You won't give up, will you?"

"Should I take that as a yes? You'll sleep in the cabin?"

"Fine, I will," he says with an uneasy smile. "Now, concentrate on the target and shoot."

Despite having memorized every movement of his muscles when he was shooting, I can't reproduce them, much less shoot with his accuracy. Or any kind of accuracy.

"So why aren't you in the Army anymore?" I ask after we call it quits for the day and gather the arrows.

Tristan hesitates. "It's a hard life. It started to take a toll on me. And... I dropped out because I wanted to spend more time with my wife. I'd been deployed almost continuously since I enlisted, so she spent the first two years of our marriage alone. Not the life she hoped for," he says. "In the short periods when I was home, things between us were tense. Very tense." His eyes search me, as if hoping I might interrupt him or switch subjects. But I don't.

I leave it up to him. If he decides not to say anything else, I won't press for more. I've already pressed enough.

"I hoped that if I returned home and took a regular job, things between us would get good again."

"And they didn't?"

He shakes his head, a bitter smile on his lips.

"Why?" I gesture to him to help me build a fire to roast the bird he shot with the arrow. The fire I build every morning to signal rescuers I no longer believe will come is already ablaze, but the way it's built doesn't make it useful for cooking.

"One reason was we had grown apart. We had spent too much time away from each other, and our experiences were different. So naturally, they shaped us in different ways. Celia was an elementary school teacher and spent her days surrounded by kids. I spent my days in Afghanistan surrounded by gunfire and people in pain or dying."

I look away from his hands when he starts plucking the bird.

"What was the other reason?"

"Hmm?"

"The other reason things didn't work out between you?"

"That other reason... that would be me." An odd noise chokes from his throat, and when he speaks again, his voice wavers. "Or rather, the post-traumatic stress disorder."

"Oh."

"I was diagnosed after I returned home. I was permanently angry and avoided people. People also avoided me, even people who had been my friends.

Some feared me. I couldn't stand hearing certain sounds. I had horrible nightmares. They used to be much, much worse than they are now. And Celia... she started wishing I'd go back in the Army again. She couldn't deal with me at all. Started avoiding me during the day. Slept in a different room at night, and then started sleeping over at a friend of hers, saying she couldn't rest. That she could still hear me."

"Did you go to counselling?"

"I did. I remember my counselor warning me that a lot of marriages like mine break up. He suggested we do couple's therapy. It took me forever to gather the courage to ask Celia to go to counselling with me. By the time I did, she was barely coming home at all. I guess it was already over for her, but I refused to see it. I had prepared this very elaborate speech, and took her to the restaurant where we'd been on our first date years before. That night she broke the news to me that she wanted a divorce."

"That's... I'm sorry... that's very sad."

"It is. It's unbelievable how fast things can go wrong. She told me she'd fallen out of love with me. And, as you correctly assumed, in love with someone else."

"Ah... "

The next few minutes pass in silence as we position the bird on the skewer, along with a few grayish, paper-tasting roots I dug up early this morning. My stomach churns at the sight of the roasting bird. It's been so long since I've eaten a proper meal. Tristan's stomach growls, too. To stave our hunger until the bird is ready, we each gulp down a few cans of water. It's lukewarm, as usual, and I'd give anything for a gulp of ice-cold water. My throat aches just at the thought of it.

Since he didn't show any signs of wanting to continue the conversation, I'm surprised when he brings up his wife again.

"They got married right after our divorce, and welcomed a child a few months later."

"Conceived while the two of you were still married?"

"Simple math would indicate that to be correct."

"How did you deal with it?"

"Badly," he says, staring at the roasting bird, his chin resting on his knees. "I sort of became a recluse for a while."

"Why didn't you return to the Army?"

"I couldn't. Despite everything, I was recovering from the trauma and didn't want to go back to square one. And I resented the Army. In a way, I felt it was responsible for everything that happened—my nightmares, losing Celia."

"Well, it was," I say.

"I don't know. I used to believe that the experiences life throws at us shape us. Now I think that it's the way we cope with what life throws our way that shapes us."

"That's an interesting way to look at things," I murmur. My mind slips back to my own dark days, after my parents passed away. Saying I didn't cope well is an understatement. But I don't want to think about my parents. I trained myself for years not to let my thoughts fly to them—to deflect my thoughts to something else when they threatened to recall something I wanted to forget. Perhaps this is why I managed so quickly to train myself not to think of

Chris ever since we crashed in this forsaken place.

"So if you don't hold the Army responsible, why didn't you reenlist?"

He shrugs. "I didn't want that life anymore. When I met Celia, I was young and full of dreams, willing to sacrifice myself for the greater good. It's easy to be generous when you are happy. I'd lost both happiness and my ability to dream. And to be honest, the Army wasn't the place to do good like I once thought it was."

"Did you always want to be in the Army?"

"I thought of becoming a doctor, too. It was either that or the military. I chose the military on my seventeenth birthday." I admired him before, for his kindness and lack of fear. Now, I admire him even more. It takes immense inner strength to make such a decision. Especially at such a young age. "When I returned from the Army, I thought about enrolling at college, then trying for med school, but I felt too old for that."

"Do you still love Celia?"

"Nah. At some point I had fallen out of love with her as well, without realizing it. I clung to her because she embodied the hope for a normal life, and then I found out that hope didn't exist anymore."

Something crosses his features... like a shadow... so thick, it's almost like a veil. I realize I've seen this expression on him before. When he shot those arrows. When he tells me good night and retreats to the cockpit. The deep frown and the pained gaze were not as pronounced, but they were there. The signs of a man retreating into his shell. No, not his shell.

His hell.

I have the inexplicable urge to say something comforting to him, to put a smile on his face, because his torment bites at me as if it were my own. Before I have the chance to give it much thought, he forces the corners of his lips into a smile and says, "So I did pilot training and started working for Chris."

"Well, good for me. Who knows how long I would have survived if someone less trained for survival had been piloting."

"I say we should go scouting for something to poison the arrow tips right after we eat," Tristan says, and I nod in agreement. But when the bird and the roots are ready, we eat so quickly our stomachs hurt worse than they did from hunger, forcing us to rest for a few hours.

"Let's get going," Tristan says. "We won't get very far today because it'll get dark in about an hour, but any progress is better than none."

I nod. "Should we take a torch with us?"

"Yes."

I go inside the plane and rip another length from my wedding dress. Its designated role is providing fabric for torches now. The first few times, it felt like ripping my skin away. Like robbing myself of the thing that preserved my hope. But now I recognize the dress still embodies hope, albeit a different hope than before. Before, it meant fulfilling my dream of getting married. Now it fulfils my hope of staying alive and keeping beasts away.

Tristan dips the strip of fabric in our last drops of liquid animal fat and then wraps it around a branch, lighting it over the fire. Then we head into the forest. It's the first time in two weeks that Tristan goes farther than just past the first few trees. It's such a relief not having to go alone again. Just seeing him in front of me, with his strong arms and confident walk, makes me feel safer than a thousand torches or weapons would.

"What are we looking for?"

Tristan purses his lips. "Not sure. There are plenty of plants here that are poisonous, but there is no way we can tell if they are poisonous enough for what we need. Let's look for plants around which there are no other plants or many insects. That's a clear sign of strong poison."

We don't come across any plants that fulfil Tristan's criteria. I doubt there is an inch of this forest that isn't covered in insects. I do point out several plants with shiny leaves and one with spines where I stung myself on the cheek a few days ago. It gave me pain that rivalled a horror trip to the dentist. Tristan isn't satisfied with any of them. Eventually I stop pointing out things and leave him to inspect the plants on his own.

Chapter 15

Aimee

We return to the plane empty-handed, and when we're about to go to sleep, Tristan heads to the cockpit.

"What are you doing? I thought we agreed that you will sleep here."

Sighing, he says, "I hoped you'd forgotten about that."

"No chance. Get whatever you need from the cockpit and come here."

I put a pillow on the seat across the aisle in the same row as mine. "There," I tell Tristan when I hear him approach. It's very dark in the plane except for the few beams of moonlight streaming through the small windows, but I've gotten so used to the darkness I can tell where everything is without a doubt. "You'll rest much better here; you'll see."

"You're the one who won't rest, Aimee. Are you sure about this?"

"Absolutely."

After Tristan leans his seat back to a lying position, I move to the back of the plane and change into the dress I use as a nightgown. Though he can't see me, I still blush when I take off my clothes. I make a mental note to go in the cockpit to change tomorrow.

I lie on my back, staring at the ceiling. It'll take hours before I fall asleep, the way it always does. "I wish I had a book or something. I used to read a novel every night until I fell asleep."

"We can tell each other stories—things that happened to us," Tristan suggests. "I mean, that's what's in a book, right, stories? You go first. I'm sure you have funnier stories than I do."

I have the feeling Tristan's suggestion has to do with his fear of falling asleep and facing his nightmares. Maybe this will help ease him to sleep.

"Okay. But I suck, I'm warning you. I once had to babysit a friend's four-year-old sister. I told her some convoluted story about how monsters were hiding under her bed and she ended up throwing a fit. Her mom couldn't calm her for hours."

"You told a four-year-old a story about monsters under the bed?" Tristan asks, bursting in a guffaw.

"Yeah. I thought it would be more interesting for her if it had a creepy aspect to it. It was a fail. So, anything you're afraid of that I should steer clear of?"

"Hmm, let's see, except my own nightmares? No, I'm good. Nothing you say can top that, I guarantee."

"What kind of story would you like to hear?"

"When did you get your favorite present?"

I smile. I thought it would be hard finding a story, but I vividly remember the details around this event. "I got it for Christmas from my parents when I was seven. Or, well, from the postman to be exact. My parents had promised me they'd be home for Christmas, but a few days before, they called to tell me they wouldn't make it. I was upset for days and refused to talk to them when they called. They were supposed to buy me the porcelain doll I had wanted for ages, and I was mad because I was sure it would take forever for them to come home and give it to me. But it arrived on Christmas day. I was so, so happy. I remember sitting in front of the TV, drinking hot chocolate while clutching the doll. It was the best Christmas ever, except I didn't have my parents. But that wasn't unusual. The holidays were a busy time for them."

"You were alone a lot when you were a kid, right?"

"Yeah. I got used to it after a while, but I still wished my parents would be around more. Especially on days like Christmas. I remember watching Christmas movies and wishing I could have a family like that. I promised myself that when I had a family, I'd spend as much time as possible with them."

"And you thought of becoming a lawyer because the working hours are so short?"

"Hey, I have excellent time management skills."

Tristan snickers. "I bet. Just like Chris. How did you two meet?"

"We've known each other forever. I don't remember a time when I didn't know him. Our parents were friends, and we lived close to each other. Chris and I were best friends long before we became lovers. Sometimes I think we were more best friends than lovers."

"We should go to sleep," Tristan says with an uncharacteristic edge in his voice.

"You're nervous, aren't you?" I ask.

He answers after a short pause. "Yes."

"Don't be." A rush of warmth fills me. I extend my arm, and the aisle between the seats is so narrow, I can touch his shoulder. He jerks away as if I've burned him. "Sorry. You don't have to be ashamed, Tristan. Or to continue to punish yourself for your bravery." He doesn't answer, but when I touch his shoulder again, he puts his own hand over mine, and for a while neither of us moves. I can tell he's more relaxed. An incomprehensible sense of fulfilment spreads through me at the thought that I contributed toward that, and that I can make his hell a bit more bearable.

Then he falls asleep. I ponder why I want so much to help him. Or do I want to help him? Maybe the answer is much simpler. Maybe I'm just starved for human touch, and I'm not doing this for his benefit at all but for my own. No, I know it's not that. His happiness simply makes me happy.

Unable to sleep, I start with a technique I often use to fall asleep: imagining a waterfall. It's supposed to relax me. I spend what feels like an hour doing that with no improvement. I give up when Tristan starts moving, mumbling in his sleep. His mumbles turn to full out screams. Ragged and desperate. They make my skin crawl. I remain on my seat at first, covering my ears. But the terror that plagues him creeps into me until my heart hammers with nauseating speed and I can no longer stand to be across the aisle. I walk over to him, wedging myself in his seat. The seats are extravagantly wide, but I realize how much weight we've both lost if we can fit in it.

"Tristan," I say, my hand hovering over his shoulder, unsure if I should shake him awake. He seems half-awake already, his eyes blinking open from time to time, unfocused. His trashing becomes wilder, more frantic, sweat beading on his forehead. The words he is muttering are incomprehensible.

"Tristan," I say again, a little louder. He grips my hand, just like he did that night he had fever. His eyes flash wide open for a few seconds and then close again. In that land between dreams and reality, he shifts closer to me until his head is almost on my chest. His grip on my hand is so tight I'm afraid it might stop my circulation, but I don't have the heart to tell him to let go. Though his clasp doesn't relax, his thrashing stops, and his breathing becomes more even.

"So many died. I couldn't save them," he whispers, his voice shaking. "Help them."

"What happened?"

"We stumbled upon a group of civilians. They weren't supposed to be there. I was instructed to lead the group to safety, but I wasn't successful. They were all killed. I see that scene again and again. It's more awful every time. In my dreams, I save them, then pick up the gun and kill them myself."

"It's just a nightmare, Tristan." I wish I could find more comforting words, because my heart breaks for him.

"No. It's a blunter version of the reality. I didn't

pull that trigger. But I did kill them."

He doesn't say anything at all afterward. He might have fallen asleep, so I try to move.

"Can you stay here for a little while?" he asks.

"Sure."

"Thanks."

After a while he falls asleep, and the nightmares don't return. How horrible it must be to face those terrifying images every night and still go through every day. A new wave of admiration swells up in me. It's been a long time since I felt this way toward someone.

I can't fall asleep, hard as I try. Returning to my seat would help, but it's out of the question. Tristan has me trapped, holding my wrist and resting his head on my chest. His other arm is around me in a very tight embrace, as if his life depended on it. Perhaps it does, and he takes strength from this just as I do when I seek strength and comfort from him when something in the forest scares the living daylights out of me. I need him to survive the horrors outside. He needs me to overcome those in his mind.

It's a good thing we can offer each other exactly the type of strength we need.

Chapter 16

Tristan

Sometimes things happen and there is no going back. I should know, I've experienced plenty of those life-changing moments. They all threw me into darkness, sending me deeper and deeper into a pit.

For once, something is happening that will pull me out of that pit—it already does.

Someone.

And now that I've found her, I can't give her up.

Chapter 17

Aimee

The first thing I do next morning is take a shower. I usually make the signal fire first and then shower, but I feel so sticky I can't stand myself anymore. Tristan is still sleeping when I get out of the plane. It has rained. The forest attains a magic hue after a rain, more so if it occurs in the morning. Mist coils through the foliage, mantling the trees and hiding the soaked floor. The sun paints rainbows almost every day. I know that because I climb to the top of a tall tree as often as I can after a rain. In the beginning I did it because I hoped to see a plane or a helicopter, but now I do it because I need to see the sun. For someone who grew up under the California sun, the few pale rays we get below the thick canopy aren't enough.

I enter our makeshift shower cabin, trying to imagine it's an exotic shower in an expensive resort, not a cubicle made out of a bunch of wood poles covered with leaves. The shower has three poles bound together on top to hold the woven water basket. If I pull at the braided rope hanging from it, water will flow from the hollow bamboo-like tube Tristan stuck in the front. But right now I need more to refresh myself than that thin stream of water. I want to overturn the basket, indulging in all of the water in one huge splash. I will replace the basket with a full one afterward. We have plenty since it rained during the night. I usually hang my clothes and towel inside the shower, but since I'm planning to unleash a cascade, I leave them outside so I don't soak them. The shower is my second favorite space after the plane. The basket is high up, so I have to jump a few times before I get a grip strong enough to overturn it. I feel like I stepped on clouds when the water pours on my hair, my face, my body, washing away the stickiness. It's warm, as always, except for a cold touch on my back... a shiver?

Or *something*.

I look once at the jet black snake curled at my feet before jumping out of the shower, screaming. I slide a few times on the muddy ground in my haste to run as far away from the shower as I can. I reach the airstairs just as Tristan descends it, and I start blabbing, shaking uncontrollably. His arms around my waist, he says something in a soothing voice, but I can't hear him over the deafening thumping in my ears.

When my pulse calms down, I manage to say, "Snake. In the shower."

"Did it bite you?"

"No, no. I just... just... kill it, please."

"Relax, Aimee. Breathe."

"I don't want to breathe," I yell, clinging to him,

fisting his shirt. "I want that thing gone from there."

"I'll take care of it. I'll just bring your towel first."

That's when I realize I'm stark naked. My boobs are pressing against his chest. My nipples have turned to pebbles. Horrified, I leap away from him, which makes everything worse because now he can see me better. But he's already seen me in all my naked glory when I was running around like a mad woman. The more I think of it, the more embarrassed I become. My cheeks burn. Scratch that. My entire body burns with shame. I cover my lady parts and my boobs until Tristan brings me the towel and the clothes, then I wrap the towel around myself. Why the hell are my nipples hard?

"The snake is not in the shower; I'll see if I can find it in the vicinity. Go inside the plane and try to calm yourself."

"Okay."

I hide inside the plane longer than calming down and changing into fresh clothes would take. Deep and utter shame keeps me rooted on my seat. I wonder if there's a way not to go out and see Tristan ever again. It's not just that he saw me, it's... how my body reacted. My hard nipples, the tingle on my skin. That wasn't because I felt ashamed.

Why then?

I play with the engagement ring on my finger, guilt drowning my feelings of shame and confusion. I remember all the other times I felt guilty, those times when it was Tristan's body that reacted inappropriately—a frantic breath, a touch that prompted him to bite his lip. I didn't understand why I felt guilty then. But I think my subconscious did. I curse loudly. An engaged woman shouldn't feel like this. Not even if she hadn't seen her fiancé in more than two months. I would have been his wife right now if this bullshit hadn't happened. I rest my head between my knees, trying very hard to picture Chris waiting for me at the altar, which is ironic since I've tried so hard to wipe that image from my mind for two months. But that image doesn't come, or any other image of him, which makes me feel even guiltier.

When I get the nerve to go outside again, Tristan has started the signal fire, as well as a regular fire next to it and is roasting something that looks delicious. I guess he's done the daily hunt already. Excellent, because I'm starving.

"Did you fall asleep?" he asks.

"Yeah, a bit," I lie.

"Good." He scans me with a worried gaze. "You didn't rest much last night, did you?"

I lie again. "Oh, it wasn't too bad." I got maybe two hours of sleep last night because of the uncomfortable position I slept in, and the heat steaming off his body was suffocating.

"I'm sorry if—"

"Let's not start that discussion again, Tristan. You have nightmares. They're not a big deal to me, just noise. But they are a big deal to you. You didn't have any more last night after I came to you. When you slept in the cockpit, you thrashed around all night. This is an improvement."

"Yeah, it is."

"Well, that is the whole point." Tristan nods as he moves the bird around over the fire. "What did you do with the snake?"

"Got rid of it. Was lying in the sun on top of the shower."

"Can we do something from preventing snakes, or anything else, falling inside the water bucket?"

"I'll come up with something, sure."

"Thanks. The food looks like it'll take a while to be ready. I'm going to search for fruit so we can eat them for dinner."

Tristan stands up abruptly. "No."

"Huh? Why? I do this every day."

"I saw some worrying paw prints around there." He points to the space between the tail of the plane and the fence.

My stomach leaps to my throat. "It got on the inside of the fence? Can you tell what it was?"

Tristan shakes his head. "It might be a jaguar."

"You said those were rare."

"Yeah, well, we already got lucky crashing on this hill above the floodwaters; I guess we aren't lucky in this department. From now on, we'll stick together at all times."

"But that's not efficient at all," I protest.

"Neither is you getting yourself killed."

"Why are you so pessimistic?" I ask, exasperated.

"I'm a realist. You have no idea how to defend yourself."

"I can climb trees," I say heatedly.

Tristan abandons all pretense of focusing on our meal and stands up, agitated. "So can every animal in this forest. Besides you freak out when you see a damn snake. How will you keep your head cool when you're face to face with a jaguar?"

"I freaked out once," I say through gritted teeth.

"Once is all it takes to make the difference between life and death. Are you actually fighting with me over going into the forest on your own? You're afraid of it."

"That's why I always try to stay close to the plane," I spit back.

"It's not up for discussion. If there's an emergency that requires just one of us to go into the forest I will go, and you wait inside the plane."

"Oh so you can go on your own, but I can't? Last time I checked, you didn't have superpowers." I try to control myself. What on earth brought on the temper? It's not because he thinks I can't defend myself. I know I can't. I take a deep breath, poking around my mind for an answer, replaying this conversation. The second the word *jaguar* pops up, I realize what brought this on. I'm just terrified— petrified that something might happen to him. It terrifies me more than the idea that something bad might happen to me. And the fact that he takes his own safety more lightly than mine furthers my apprehension.

"I can defend myself, Aimee," he says in a more measured tone.

I back off, drawing a few deep breaths. "Okay, I'm being ridiculous. You are right, of course. It's dangerous to run on my own when there might be a jaguar around. But we have to be reasonable. I went by myself into the forest countless times when your back was hurting, and nothing happened."

"We had no other choice. Maybe you got lucky. At any rate, this is a risk we can't take. We'll coordinate everything so we waste as little time as possible. When you search for fruit, I can look for poisonous plants or eggs."

"All right," I say, still unsatisfied. Tristan puts his hand under my chin, raising it. His touch sends an electric jolt through me, making my entire body heat up. Whether it's the heated discussion or another kind of heat, I don't want to know, but I take a step back just the same.

"The only way I'm going to allow you to go off on your own is if you learn to shoot straight," he says, and the determination in his eyes is almost unsettling. Nodding toward the tree with the target he says, "The bow and arrows are there. Practice until our meal is ready."

I groan, but do as he says. He's right. I need to be able to defend myself. I need to get better at this. My resolution starts to dissolve twelve arrows into my practice. No more than one has hit the target. I can hardly concentrate on shooting, and every time I stare at the target for longer than a few seconds, I get dizzy. So maybe going into the forest today to climb trees in search for eggs and fruit wouldn't have been such a good idea, jaguars aside. The fact that I slept even less than usual is blurring my vision and diminishing my focus. That can mean the difference between stepping on the right branch or the wrong one and falling from the tree, since the nests are on the higher branches.

"Your stance is wrong again," Tristan says from behind me.

"Argh," I exclaim. "Damn it, Tristan. Announce yourself, will you? I don't need a heart attack."

"Sorry, didn't want to scare you." Putting his hand on my belly, he says, "You don't have any pressure here."

"I... I know, it's just..." I take a deep breath, trying hard not to acknowledge how his touch affects me. What the hell is it with me today? He's touched me like this dozens of times before, and *he* was the one who seemed affected by it. Not me.

"I can't concentrate."

"You didn't rest last night; I knew it."

Time to lie again. "No, it's not that. I just... I'm not good at it."

Tristan looks unconvinced, but doesn't insist. "Let's eat. You can practice afterward."

But I manage to skip another training session after the meal, because we decide to go together searching for eggs and fruit and wood. I let Tristan do the climbing, and I stick to collecting wood, since it requires least attention. By the time we are back it's too dark to do anything except take a shower—after Tristan checks the water basket for any unwanted guests. While he showers I go to inspect the paw print. I hold a torch close to the ground until I find it. And then I wish I hadn't. It's enormous. How big is this beast? The hair at the back of my neck stands on end as I try to imagine it. Tristan joins me when he gets out of the shower.

"Scary, isn't it?"

"By all means. Why did it come here?"

"Hard to say." He shrugs. "Maybe it's just lost or..."

"Or what?"

"Maybe it's a jaguar inspecting this place to see if it's suitable to become its territory."

"Could there be more of them?"

"Nah... jaguars are solitary creatures. They don't

run in packs. Of course, if it's a female with cubs, and the cubs are bigger than cute kittens, we'd have a small pack on our hands."

"What would happen then?"

His expression darkens. "We'd have to leave immediately."

"But you said that was something you'd consider only as a last resort." My knees turn weak. "The forest is still underwater."

"That is a last resort. No amount of arrows, even poisoned ones, will help if more jaguars come. We'd starve hiding inside the plane, and we wouldn't be able to come out."

"I'd rather die from lack of food than become food."

"I'll take care of you, Aimee. I promise. Let's go inside now; it's too dark." Without warning, he puts his arms around me in a tender embrace. From the plethora of feelings striking me in this moment— heat, guilt, confusion—most powerful is the feeling that I *belong* here in his arms.

I feel at home in them.

We stay like this for a long time, and then we head toward the plane.

As I climb the airstairs I ask him, "The odds of a female with cubs isn't that great, is it?"

"Not sure," Tristan says from behind me. "I think this is one of the few areas of the Amazon that doesn't get flooded in the rainy season. This place must look pretty attractive. But we were lucky until now; maybe we'll stay lucky."

His answer doesn't calm me in the slightest. I stop before entering the plane, straining my ears to discern anything that sounds more ominous than usual in the permanent buzz of the rainforest.

Nothing.

Maybe Tristan's right. But what if our luck has come to an end?

"Your turn to tell a story," I say as I yawn in my seat, preparing to go to sleep. I am so exhausted, I won't have any trouble falling asleep tonight.

"I told you I don't have any good ones. The Army isn't full of cheerful stories."

"Is this why all your poems are so dark? Because of the Army?"

"Yes. I wasn't much into reading before I enrolled. During a short break at home, before I left for Afghanistan, I bought a magazine, and it included a small book of poems as a freebie. Anniversary something. It was a collection from various poets—they were all, *dark*, as you call them. That got me started. It sounds weird, but they were comforting."

"Why?"

"I was surrounded by so much pain and misery that my own thoughts became very dark. So dark that I started to worry. It was comforting to realize that darkness can lead to beauty. Like poems. Why are the ones you quote so cheerful?"

"Those are the only ones I remember." I shrug, feeling ashamed. "No deeper meaning."

"Well, the fact that you only remember those means something."

Maybe he's expecting me to understand what he means, but I don't. And I don't ask.

Instead I say, "You still owe me a story. Tell me a pre-Army story. What made you choose Army? I mean, there must have been a reason. You didn't just wake up on the morning of your seventeenth birthday and decided to do it, did you?"

"I pretty much did. When I was a kid my favorite hero was a character in a comic book who was a commander in the Army, so I wanted to be one too. I guess the idea just stuck as I grew up. I never wanted to be anything else."

"That's sweet; you got to follow your dream."

He hesitates. "Some dreams are better left unfollowed. They can turn into nightmares."

I don't have an answer for that. What can I tell a man who followed his childhood dreams only to have reality beat them out of him?

"I bet you were a little hero even when you were young. Come on... I'm sure you'll come up with something."

"I don't know about being a hero, but I was very daft. I almost drowned once. This girl was crying because her dog fell into a lake, so I jumped in after it."

"Why do you think that was daft?"

"Because dogs can swim better than people. The dog ended up saving me."

"How old were you?"

"Eleven."

I try to wrap my mind around someone doing that at the age of eleven. The most I can remember about that age was throwing a fit if the present my parents sent me every two weeks from wherever they were didn't arrive on time. Yeah, I was spoiled.

Some people are born to see what matters in life. They can sense it. Like my parents. I always admired their ability to put everything aside, including me, in order to concentrate on their work.

"It was foolish," Tristan says, laughing through the darkness.

"Not at all. It was very admirable of you." I bury my head in my pillow. I'm grateful there are people like him whose natural instinct is to do good for others. It's almost a sin that he hasn't received the kindness he deserves in return. My last thought before I fall asleep is that maybe I'll manage to accomplish that, in some limited way, in this wilderness.

I wake up to screams. Cold panic grips me, convinced that the jaguars are upon us. Then I come to my senses. It's just Tristan's nightmares. I approach him cautiously, shaking him awake. He smiles when he sees me, though his eyes still have a haunted look to them.

"Can you sit next to me for a while?" he murmurs.

"Sure," I say, though I'm more uneasy than I was last night when I gave the same answer. After the incident today and my body's decision to act so outrageously, I'm not sure I should be so close to him. But what can I tell him? *Sorry, Tristan, I have to back off helping you through your nightmares because my nipples decided to turn to pebbles today and my skin turns to burning coal when I am too close to you*. Asides from it being ridiculous, it would be selfish of me to back off and unfair to him.

As I sit next to him and he gazes at me intensely with his endlessly dark eyes, his chest rising and falling in the same lightning-quick succession as mine, I remember the other times when my proximity seemed to have the same effect on him that his proximity now has on me. I try to stay just far enough from him that our bodies don't touch.

Feeling his hot breath on my skin is unavoidable though.

"You want to talk about the nightmare?" I ask.

"No, not tonight."

"Okay."

"When I was in the Army, I dreamed about being home, eating my omelette in the morning without worrying I might not make it to the next day." So that's why something as simple as an omelette is his favorite meal. That's why he notices details others don't. Like how I drink my coffee, or that I change my hair color often.

"When I got home I didn't dream anymore. I just got nightmares. I wish I could have a dream instead of a nightmare just once. I haven't dreamed about something peaceful in a long time."

"What would you like to dream about?"

"No idea. Never thought about it. I just don't want to be back in Afghanistan every time I close my eyes."

"Hmm, you should try visualizing what you want to dream instead of what you don't want to dream."

"That sounds like something a therapist would say."

"Umm... I read it in a bridal magazine. It was advice to avoid bad dreams about all the preparations."

A guffaw reverberates from his chest, like I suspected it would.

"Sounds shallow, doesn't it?"

"Nah, it's just funny how much women can stress themselves over weddings. Some of the native tribes in the Amazon used to have very simple ceremonies to celebrate weddings. They would just tattoo each other's name or symbols on their bodies."

"That can't be true," I say, shuddering. The thought of getting a tattoo always baffled me. It hurts and it's permanent. Why do it?

"Yeah it is. When we get back to a place with Internet, you can check it."

"You can bet; that'll be my first concern if we ever get back to civilization," I mock him.

"Did that magazine advice work?"

"No idea. I didn't have nightmares, I just read it. But a friend of mine who got married last year swore it helped her, though it took a bit of time until that happened."

"All right, I'll try it," he says, though by the tone of his voice I can tell he doesn't trust a technique for bridezillas to help him drive away nightmares of war bombs. I don't blame him.

"I suppose it takes training, just like me with the arrows. I hope you'll get better at it quicker than I am with the arrows."

"You will get better at that," he says with conviction. "Even if I have to stand behind you and correct you every day for hours. It's even more important now than it was before."

"Thanks. Let me know if there's anything I can do to help you with... umm."

"You already are." He turns to me, coming closer. He takes so much time to form the next words that I almost think he will change his mind and say nothing at all. But when he speaks, I realize why it took him so long. "It's so much better when you're next to me. I first noticed it that night I had a fever." It's an admission that costs him. A lot. Because he can't take it back. During the day, it's easy for him to say he can go back to sleeping alone in the cockpit.

But at night, when the horrors he's trying so hard to forget torture him, he can't pretend.

"I noticed that you were still that night when I was close to you, but I wasn't sure if the fever had just knocked you out or not. Why didn't you say anything?"

"I was ashamed. Still am."

"Don't be."

"I'd hate to make you feel uncomfortable just so I can—"

"Why, because that would be selfish? Tristan, you've earned the right to be selfish for two lifetimes. And for the record, I don't think you're being selfish at all."

He watches me for a long time before he asks, "Then will you stay here next to me? Even after I fall asleep?"

A shiver runs up my spine as I answer, because I've never felt this needed in my life. "I will. I promise."

"Good."

"Now, come up with something nice to dream about," I urge.

To my astonishment, he chuckles. "Oh, I know what I can use to start my dream training."

"I'm all ears."

"I'm hoping for a mental replay of your naked dance today," he says, grinning.

"Tristan! And I had deemed you a gentleman because you didn't mention it."

"It was fantastic."

I pinch his chest playfully with my fingers. And regret it. Touching him this little is enough to give me goose bumps on my arms. Goose bumps he can't miss, even though there's scarce light, because his other hand shoots to my arm, pinching me back. He sucks in his breath when he feels my skin under his fingers. I wish now there was not even the glow of moonlight in the plane, so I couldn't see the glint of desire in his eyes.

"Promise me you won't think about that," I say, praying that he'll take my reaction as a manifestation of my embarrassment.

Pulling back his hand he says, "Hey, that's not fair. You said I could be selfish."

"But that's my body you are talking about. I forbid you to dream about it."

"You'll never know," he says.

But I do know. Because when he falls asleep, he starts mumbling again about bombs and everything being his fault, and it's not until he rests his head on my chest, slinging his arms around me, that he calms down. I don't sleep for one minute the rest of the night, guilt chocking me. I stare at my diamond ring until I get teary.

Chapter 18

Aimee

"Can we slow down a bit, please?" I pant a week later, during our daily raid in the forest for food. "I need to rest a bit."

"I'd rather we got to the plane, Aimee."

"Just one minute, please."

"Fine," he scrutinizes me, as if expecting me to collapse at his feet any minute now, which is possible. "Rest here a few minutes until I collect some more fruit. I saw some ripe ones up there." He points to a tree to our right. "I'll keep an eye on you."

"I have no doubt," I say in a whisper that's covered by the squawk of some kind of animal hiding in the tree. The sounds of life scurrying in every direction, on every inch of the forest don't frighten me as much as they used to. Not the croaks, or shrills, or the chorus of other indistinguishable buzzing noises. I can't quite say the same about the howls of predators, but I'm trying to channel that fear into learning how to defend myself.

The minute Tristan turns his back to me and starts climbing the tree, I drop the fruit I'm carrying, rest against a tree, and draw deep breaths. I close my eyes. I can't go on like this. My insomnia is worse. Between Tristan's nightmares and my consuming guilt, I never manage to sleep more than an hour a night. I can't concentrate, and I'm paying for it. Yesterday I stumbled over some roots and cut my left foot, so now I'm limping. Tristan insisted he put antibiotics on it so that wiped out half of our meagre supply. If something worse happens, we have next to nothing to treat ourselves with. I need to sleep more, or I'll become a liability soon. What with a fresh set of jaguar prints we discovered yesterday inside our fence, I can't afford that. The good part is that we are almost sure it's just that one jaguar. The bad part is that since he keeps coming back, he must have found the place interesting. Tristan still insists we should do all tasks together, and I'm not against the idea anymore. Whenever he disappears from my eyesight, even for just a few seconds, I'm terrified that something might have happened to him.

We haven't yet found a strong enough poison. Tristan tried countless plants that looked poisonous last week, taking their leaves and making concoctions out of them. He tested the poisoned arrows on a few poor, unsuspecting birds. The results weren't great. In fact, not even good.

"Aimee."

I startle, opening my eyes. I dozed off.

"Are you okay?" Tristan asks.

"Yeah, unless an army of ants crept up my arms again." This is a lesson I've learned the hard way: never sit on the forest floor or rest against a tree for more than a few seconds. Insects and reptiles hide on tree bark, ready to strike when they get the chance.

"Gather your fruit, I'll carry everything else. We should go back."

I unhitch myself from the tree, inspecting my arms. Not one insect or sign of a sting. Whew. "This must be some kind of miracle." I bend down to gather the fruit I dropped at my feet, when the tree bark catches my attention. It's white, as if someone painted it. And there are no insects on it. I take out my pocket knife and make a long cut into the bark. It's superficial, but a dark brown liquid starts coming out of the crack, as if the tree were bleeding.

"Tristan, come look at this."

He narrows his eyes as he inspects it. "No insects on it," he murmurs.

"Exactly."

In unison, we both look at the ground. There are some plants growing around the tree, but not nearly as many as usual. The sap of the tree must be poisonous. Very.

"Let's collect this. It might just be what we need." Watching me, he adds, "I'll take you back to the plane and then come back to do it."

"Don't be ridiculous. It'll be quicker with the two of us. Let's just get it over with."

I dig my knife into the tree before Tristan starts protesting. His overprotectiveness is moving but also worrying. He's putting himself at risk by being preoccupied looking after me instead of looking where he steps. The best thing I could do is stay inside the plane and let him come back to the forest alone. I wouldn't be of any use in case of an attack, quite the contrary. But I can't bring myself to leave him out of my sight.

We spend the next hour cutting into the bark and collecting the sap in two small baskets I weave together on the spot. I make sure to keep my distance from Tristan while we do it. Touching him, even by accident, still sets my skin ablaze. Worse, it makes me tingle in places I have no business tingling. Since I don't know what to make of that, I concentrate on the guilt; which follows me permanently. It's strongest at night when I sleep next to him, and there is no escape from his touch. The guilt isn't from the tingling I feel at his touch. It's from craving it.

As much as I dread it, I'm also looking forward to the moment when he asks me to spend the night next to him. Last night was the first time I stayed at his side without him asking me first. He recounted his nightmare numerous times, each time adding more gruesome details, until his words painted images so real they terrified me almost as much as they terrified him. I came to understand why this particular event, of all the horrors he witnessed, marked him. He made it out alive, but none of the civilians he was supposed to protect did. Survivor guilt. Talking about it seems to help. He's making progress. Real progress. His nightmares are shorter, and it's easier to wake him up. That's why I have to stay by his side. To help him.

Or so I'm telling myself.

When we're back at the plane, Tristan dips the points of two arrows in the liquid we collected and starts looking for a victim to try it on. He finds a bird sitting on a lower branch, picking around at its plumage. Tristan sets the arrow inside the bow and positions himself for a shot. My stomach pulls together until I'm positive it's the size of a nut when he releases the arrow. In less than a fraction of a second the poor bird drops dead. I swing forward, puking.

"Aimee!"

"I'm fine. Go away."

I usually turn away when he shoots something, but I wasn't quick enough. I go sit at our makeshift eating place. Tristan sits in front of me a while later, handing me a can of heated water. I rinse my mouth until it's clean.

"Well, we've found our poison," he says.

"I kind of got that." I hope we won't have to use it. We've been here for two months and one week and haven't needed it so far.

"I'll make us some small pouches so we can carry the poison with us in case we need it."

I frown. "Why not just dip the arrows in the poison and carry them around like that?" My shot is still lame, but I'd feel safer if we did that.

"It's dangerous. If we were to accidentally stab ourselves..."

"Oh, yeah. You're right."

"I'll make us dinner from the fruit we gathered."

"I'm not sure I can manage to eat tonight, but you can make something for yourself. I still want to finish washing the pile of clothes we were washing before we headed into the forest."

We wash our clothes with a regularity that is almost maniacal, but they still have an unpleasant smell. Not sweat. Tristan and I shower three or four times a day, because of the heat and humidity. I suspect the clothes smell because we're washing them with nothing more than water since the shower gel is gone. I almost fall asleep twice while washing, so I give up before I finish the pile, telling Tristan that I'm going to bed early. It's almost dark anyway. Tristan enters the cabin just after I finish changing. He changes in the cockpit, returning when I'm about lie down.

Tristan sits on the edge of his seat. "Aimee?" There is a hesitancy in his voice that unsettles me.

"Yes."

"Umm, what would you say to sleeping next to me right from the start?"

"Huh?"

"You come over here afterward anyway. Maybe I won't have nightmares at all if you're here when I fall asleep."

Logically, his suggestion makes sense. I always end up spending the entire night beside him anyway. But even though I agree, something tells me it's not okay. I just can't pinpoint what isn't right about it.

I slide next to him. It's impossible to avoid skin-to-skin contact, and his touch burns me as intensely as ever. Neither of us says anything; we just face the ceiling. In this silence, it clicks. It feels wrong because it's so intimate.

"It's your turn to tell a story," he says.

"I'm too tired to come up with one."

I feel him shift next to me and then he turns on one side, looking at me. That doesn't help the feeling of wrongness at all.

"You don't sleep well at all, do you?"

"No," I admit.

"I'm sorry." He pushes himself up in a sitting position. "I'll go back to the cockpit."

"No, Tristan!" I grab his arm. "Don't. I'll fall asleep eventually. I shouldn't have told you."

He leans back on his elbows, and without looking in my direction says, "I noticed you weren't sleeping well a few days ago, but I didn't say anything. I wanted to be selfish and keep you here. But I don't want to harm you. It's just that it's so much better when you are next to me. "

His confession tugs at my heartstrings. "You're not harming me, Tristan. I've been battling insomnia forever. It's gotten worse here. I can handle it. Come on, lie down and try to sleep. I'm glad it's getting better for you." He does lie down, but he doesn't seem too keen on sleeping.

"I don't want you to resent me. If you start down that path, you'll want to avoid me, but there is nowhere to run away here."

"Neither of those things will happen."

"If I could find a way for them to forgive me for not saving them, maybe I could live with myself," he whispers.

"You wouldn't. Even if every single one of them could tell you it's not your fault. You have to forgive yourself, Tristan, if you want peace. It's all on you."

He smiles softly. "Tell me a secret."

"What?"

"You know mine. It's only fair that I know one of yours."

"I'll pass, thanks."

"Tell me," he beckons. "It weighs less on you after you share it with someone, I promise. You just proved that to me."

His words erase any chance for sleep, so I turn on my side, too, facing him. The thought of a shared secret weighing less is too tempting. I give in. "Well, remember how I told you I used to want to be like my parents, and do what they were doing before they passed away?"

"Yes."

"The truth is, the prospect of being like them frightened me. I felt I'd never have the strength to leave those I love behind for months at a time and travel to foreign places. I admired them; they were my heroes, and I wanted to do something good like they did, but I didn't feel strong enough for that lifestyle. So I suppose my decision to change careers wasn't entirely driven by pain."

Tristan doesn't reply so I check to see whether he's fallen asleep, but his eyes are open. Maybe he thinks I'm a coward. I squirm in shame. I was better off keeping my secret.

"You were looking at it from a wrong perspective," Tristan says.

"What?"

"You were looking up to your parents because you thought what they did was noble, right? Helping others?"

"Yeah..." I confirm, not sure where he's heading.

"You didn't have to literally step into their shoes to do that. Each person has unique strengths. You could have achieved what you wanted by using your unique strength."

"And what is my strength?" I challenge.

"Listening to people," he says in a surprised tone. "And not just that. Empathizing with them."

"Tristan, you're overestimating me a bit. Just because we've been talking—"

"It's not just me. Kyra talked about you a lot, after her husband dumped her. She said you were very kind, listened to her. Gave her good advice."

I remember that time in Kyra's life. Her husband left her about a year ago, and she transformed from her bubbly self to a moping mess. I tried to help her the best I could, but never had the impression I'd succeeded.

"You have an inner strength that few people have. And you know how to give it to others. You could help people in your own way. Taking care of them one by one. Like you do with me. I've told you things I haven't told anyone. Not even the counsellor. In a way, I've given you a part of my past—of me—that I have never given to anyone. I'm not used to making myself vulnerable."

I've never heard anyone talk so openly about their feelings. I have no idea how to respond, and it seems that he's expecting me to. I rack my tired brain to come up with something else to talk about.

"What did the natives use to tattoo themselves in the marriage ceremony? Did it hurt more than getting a regular tattoo?" I blurt out, remembering what he told me a week ago. *Smooth, Aimee. Really smooth way to change the subject.*

"I have no idea," Tristan answers, confusion dripping from his voice.

"But doing something like that if it hurts is barbaric. Well, I always kind of thought getting a tattoo was barbaric. And what if you want to get rid of it?"

"They don't plan to remove it at all. That's the whole point of it. I think it's beautiful to give yourself to someone so utterly and completely."

My breath catches. Maybe if he hadn't told me a few minutes ago that he's given a part of himself to me that he had never given to anyone else, I'd think nothing of this. As it is... I can't help thinking that this... whatever this is... means so much more to him than I thought. But I'm not sure I'm ready to find out what it means. His eyes have an intense glint to them that ripples through me. When I can't hold his gaze any longer, I turn around and say, "Good night."

Tristan falls asleep before me, his even breathing filling the cabin. I manage to convince myself I'm overreacting and almost fall asleep too. Then he slings an arm around my waist, moving close to me. Too close. Feeling every inch of his body pegged to mine is excruciating.

His breath feathers on my nape, his strong chest muscles press against my back. And his lower body—no, I won't go there. But my body doesn't need my permission to torture me. A strong, almost painful need awakens deep inside my core. I can't quench it, hard as I try. Not even guilt can quench it. Tomorrow I will tell Tristan I can't do this anymore. I will sleep in my place and only come to him if he needs me. We are both confused enough as it is. Me—unable to control my body, and he... that look in Tristan's eyes spoke of feelings he shouldn't have for me. I've let this go too far. But it's not like sleeping next to him will make any difference.

But it does make a difference. Tristan sleeps the entire night without waking up once. It's me who has a nightmare this time. I wake up panting, with tears in my eyes. In my nightmare, we were attacked by a pack of wild beasts, and Tristan helped me up a tree that had no lower branches so the animals couldn't climb it. Then he got torn apart by the beasts. When I realize he's next to me, unharmed, I snuggle up in his arms and weep again, this time with joy. I wonder, why the sudden dream? Tristan has gone to great lengths to protect me these past weeks.

As I drift off to sleep again, a frightening awareness wedges its way into my mind. I thought the bond between us here in the rainforest was one of friendship. But maybe it's more. Maybe I feel more than I think for this man who's not only the strongest person I've met, but who also seems more determined to keep me alive than himself.

Chapter 19

Aimee

The next days we sink into the deepest hell there must be, because we find fresh paw prints inside the fence each morning. And then a second set of prints, which is just as large as the first ones. Tristan was right. It's a female jaguar with at least one cub. And the cub is no longer the size of a cute kitten, but a deadly size. There is no sight of the beasts during the day, but they roam around at night. They knock over our wood supply and drink our water. Tristan suggests leaving once or twice, but neither of us thinks it's a very good idea. We climb down the hill regularly; the water level is still very high. We'd be advancing at a slow pace, and it'd be hard to build a shelter during the night. Then, on the morning marking two months and two weeks since we crashed, the paw prints vanish. Another week has passed since then, and we still look for them every morning and check the fence for holes, but there are no fresh holes or paw prints. Maybe the jaguar female and her cub (I refuse to think plural—cubs) were just passing by this area.

Tristan still checks the fence every morning, but I've stopped going with him. He also does one last round in the evening after we eat, carrying a torch, and that's where he is right now; whereas I'm curled in my seat, chewing my lip. Tonight I'm trying to muster the courage to tell him what I couldn't say this past week: I don't want to sleep so close to him anymore. Jaguars aside, I've been through my own personal hell. While I've been sleeping longer than one hour a night, sleeping next to him is becoming more torturous night by night. He's better now, his nightmares few and far between. There's no reason to continue this.

"No traces," Tristan announces, entering the plane. "I'll go change and be back in a minute." He disappears in the cockpit without glancing at me. He hasn't seen that I'm not lying in his seat, but in my own.

But he does see five minutes later when he returns. He stops in front of the seats. I had all this speech prepared how it's best if I sleep here, but under his hurtful gaze, the words I manage to get out are, "I want to sleep in my spot tonight, Tristan. It's just so warm in here. It's even warmer when we're so close together."

He reads right through my excuse. "I see. All right. Sleep tight, then." Without another word, he's off to sleep. I try to do the same, without success. I start my old technique of imagining a waterfall—I haven't had to use it since I've slept by Tristan's side. I start painting the image behind my eyelids when his nightmare begins. Wild. Loud. Desperate. In a heartbeat, I'm right next to him.

"Tristan," I whisper. His nails graze the leather chair in his relentless thrashing, and I can't seem to be able to wake him. I pin my knees on the chair at his sides, trapping him beneath me, restricting his ability to move. Then I put my palms on each of his cheeks, and call his name louder. When he opens his eyes, the moonlight shines over the terror and pain in his eyes. It tears at me, guilt branching out from deep inside my chest. I shouldn't have left his side tonight.

"Just stay with for a little while, please. I need you so much, Aimee." The sound of my name from his mouth awakens something in me that has me writhing in a blazing torture. It's doing things to me it shouldn't do.

"Shh, okay. I'll stay. I know it helps having someone."

"Not someone. You. You make the memories bearable, the present better. You have an unbelievably strong will to keep going, even if you don't know where you're heading, hoping you'll find something worthy at the end of the road. You have an inherent ability to pick up the good on the way—those that give you strength, the happy things, like your poems—and you go on. You pass that strength onto others, even if it costs you sleep and peace.

"I used to hate waking up every morning. Now I look forward to every day, even though we're stuck in this place. Because it means one more day with you." He caresses my lips with his thumb. I open my mouth, but he shakes his head. "Don't say anything, please."

For a long moment, we are silent, our gazes locked. I breathe in his hot breaths, tension crackling in the short distance between our lips. Then he pulls me into a kiss. The touch of his lips on mine electrifies me, shimmer after shimmer coursing through my nerve endings. His tongue takes mine in a primal claim. Icy shivers splinter my skin, and at the same time, fire awakens deep within me. I've never been kissed like this. Ferociously, with absolute, desperate need. I try to temper the heated emotions building inside me. I try to remember it's wrong. But that fleeting thought is drowned by the heat igniting his lips and hands, and I surrender. Tristan deepens the kiss until I'm out of breath. I become aware of his hard chest muscles, of every line and every ridge, as my hands roam wildly with a greed I don't recognize. His hands graze my body, traveling from my back to my thighs, spreading the fire in my center; I'm convinced it will consume me. With a jolt, he pulls me even closer to him, so I'm all but straddling him. His fingers fumble with my hair, as his blessed mouth cradles mine, coaxing a whimper from me.

And then I snap out of it. I push myself away, breathless, flushed, and ashamed. I spring to my feet, taking refuge in my seat, guilt seeping into me like a poisoned arrow. I try to concentrate on the sound of the torrential rain outside. It's pouring. I curl in a fetal position. The realization of what I have done grows, fuelling the guilt, until I can't stand being in my own skin anymore.

Chapter 20

Tristan

Staying away from her tears at me. But I know trying to talk to her, or comforting her, would only make it worse. I know what she's thinking about, because I am too. *Him*. This is one hell of a way to thank him for helping me.

But there is no going back after this.

I will fight for her.

Chapter 21

Aimee

I wake up as light leaks into the plane. I jolt into a sitting position, remembering the events of last night. Tristan is still sleeping in his reclined seat. I get dressed and quickly run out of the plane. Once outside, I don't stop. I keep running, my feet sinking deep into the mud formed by the rain last night. Making a run for it, yes, that's what I need. But where? There's nowhere to run.

No matter.

I keep going, keep moving. If I run fast enough—far enough—this suffocating bubble in my throat must fade, maybe even vanish. And with it, my guilt too. But something inexplicable happens. Instead of diminishing, the bubble grows in size, until even the tiniest of breaths become unbearable. I can't leave the guilt behind. Because it's not Tristan I want to run away from.

It's myself.

So I stop, resting my hands on my knees, nauseous

from my sprint. The sight of my diamond ring brings tears to my eyes. I close them, desperately trying to conjure an image of Chris. But the months I've trained myself not to think of him render my efforts useless. My memories of Chris are fond, but distant. They pale in comparison to the ones I've collected here, their intensity molded by the danger of the forest and the presence of a man who smothers me with kindness and awakes a fire I never knew existed. A man whose pain I can feel as if it's my own. Every memory, every experience before this, before *him*, pales. But the guilt doesn't pale.

What have I done? How did I allow things to come to this? Why did I give in last night? The answer slings itself through my mind, cutting and unforgiving: because I wanted it so much. Needed it, even. Shaking, I dig in my memories, trying to make sense of this, searching for signs I should have seen this coming.

Once I start remembering, the signs are everywhere.

All those times I wanted to comfort him, when I unintentionally questioned him about things that were painful for him to remember.

My elation at seeing him happy.

The terror I felt—still do—at the thought that something bad may happen to him. Friendship may have prompted these feelings once, but not anymore. When exactly I crossed that barrier, I do not know. But I certainly crossed it, because what I feel is so much more powerful. Shatteringly so. The guilt strangling me is a confirmation of the nature of my feelings.

Suddenly I can't bear being out here by myself.

I straighten up. Where the hell am I? I don't recognize the trees around me. I'm certain I haven't been here before. How long have I been running? My heart hammers against my ribcage. I grab at my waistband for my pocketknife, but I don't have it with me. Damn it. This was stupid. I didn't take the spear or my bow, either. I look around, searching for something that looks familiar through the trees. Nothing. I break out in a sweat, trying to ignore the panic and find my way back. I swallow hard, willing to calm myself. I came down the hill, so as long as I go back up, I should at least be going in the right direction. I lower my eyes to the forest floor and see my own footprints in front of me. I follow the trail, grateful for the rain last night. It takes me a long time to get back. I try to walk on my tiptoes, stopping now and again to look around for any signs that a beast might be following me. I feel vulnerable without my knife. After a while, I pick up a fallen branch. If worst come to worst, I'll defend myself with it. Some of the leaves freckling the ground aren't covered in mud, and I see them in more detail. The rich colors and shapes put a smile on my face. Nature paints more vividly and inventively than any man's imagination ever will.

Something catches my eye: a pack of white, beautiful flowers. Orchids. An irrational joy overcomes me seeing the familiar flower, as if the florist back in L.A. has sprung from behind a tree, asking me if I want them packed in silver or pink paper. I pick as many as I can, using my T-shirt as a holder. I also pick up some wood to use as an excuse for being away in case Tristan is already up when I return. I hope he isn't… he'll throw a fit because I left on my own.

But he isn't awake.

So I start my daily routine, showering, setting up the signal fire, and digging for some roots to eat for breakfast. I also search for fruit. Heavy dew mantles everything outside, draping the bark of trees, making the climb for fruit more difficult. The drops of water seem to bring out a plethora of tiny neon-blue lizards with orange striped backs that scamper up and down the bark. I have to be careful not to touch them while I climb. I touched one my first week here, and developed an annoying rash. After a lecture from Tristan on being more careful because even frogs can be poisonous in the rainforest, I'm not taking any chances.

I stay close to the fence in my search. This kind of physical work is what I need right now, keeping busy enough to not drown in guilt. It doesn't exhaust me, so I can contemplate how to handle the situation. The cleverest thing I come up with is acting as if nothing happened. I hope he'll play along.

I'm in front of the fire, about to roast the roots, when Tristan says, "Why didn't you wake me up?" I twist the ring on my finger, like I've done all morning. Tristan has an uncharacteristic grin on his face, then his gaze drops to my ring and his grin dissipates. I turn away from him, concentrating on the roots. For a long time he doesn't say anything. The silence becomes unbearable, so I make the process of roasting the roots as loud as possible. After they are done, I put two on a folded leaf for him, and keep two for myself. I hand him the leaf without looking at him and make a point of staring at the fire while we eat.

"Are those *orchids* by the shelter?"

"Yes. I found them by a tree farther away from here. They're beautiful."

"You went out alone today, didn't you?" he asks briskly. "Don't you understand how dangerous this is, Aimee?"

I swallow hard, looking away. He's right, of course. In hindsight, my flight this morning seems even more idiotic given we could be surrounded by jaguars. The fact that we haven't found fresh paw prints doesn't mean they have left.

"I needed time alone." The words tumble out of my mouth before I can stop them. Tristan turns pale. I hold my breath.

"No problem," he says, fixing me with his gaze. The intensity of his eyes spears me like a flaming arrow. I lose myself in his gaze. The same need from last night burns in them. And something else, too. Pain. This is an opportunity to discuss last night. He wants to. Like the coward I am, I choose to remain silent. When Tristan speaks again, the pain in his voice is devastating. "The next time you want to be alone, stay in the plane and tell me to get lost. If it comes to that, I can handle myself better out here than you can. I'm going to check the fence for any holes and strengthen it."

I remain seated on the trunk, too stunned for words. I just hurt him—really hurt him—and all he can worry about is my safety. A new feeling spreads its wings inside me. Shame.

I spring to my feet, following him to the fence.

"No. I'll do this." His tone is cutting. His dismissal hurts me, but I deserve it. Maybe he needs time alone too. Or maybe he just can't stand being close to me.

I stay out of his sight, wondering what he's doing at the fence. He hasn't found any holes in it during his daily inspections, so there isn't anything to fix. He must be trying to stay away from me. When I can't stand being alone anymore, I go searching and find Tristan on the other side of the plane, hunched over a portion of the fence. I don't see what he's doing, but when he steps back, my heart stops. There is a giant hole in the fence.

"When did this appear?" I ask.

He straightens up without looking at me. "It must have been in the night. It wasn't here yesterday."

The paw prints in front of the hole clarify what kind of animal caused the hole. A jaguar.

"I don't understand, there haven't been any new holes in the fence for a few days..." When Tristan doesn't say anything, a somber doubt creeps in. "Or have there been, Tristan?"

"There have been two holes in the last two days, though no paw prints have been inside the fence."

"Why didn't you tell me?"

Sighing, he says, "Because I didn't want to worry you."

His answer melts me. I place my hand on his shoulder. He winces, but I don't remove it. "Don't keep things away from me, okay? We're a team."

"A team," he repeats.

"Yes. A team. What do we do now?"

Tristan purses his lips, lost in thought. "Strengthen the entire fence. Let's put another row of branches and leaves all around it, doubling it."

"And that will keep them at bay?" I ask.

"It'll be better than what we have now."

"Can we put some plants with spines on the outside?" An idea strikes me. "Sort of mimicking a barbed-wire fence?"

"That's a good idea. Except they'll dry off quickly and won't be as useful anymore."

"Not if we uproot them and replant them here."

"It'll take a lot of time."

"I don't have a better idea."

Tristan considers my words for a few moments. "We'll double it with branches today. That will take us the whole day. We'll start to plant spine plants tomorrow."

"Sounds like a plan."

We venture into the forest to gather branches. We have a hefty reserve of wood for fire, but that's not good enough for the fence.

Tristan was right, doubling the fence does take up the entire day. It's hard work and we do it more meticulously than the first time. I remember the day we first put the fence up, the day I decided to get closer to Tristan, and started firing my never-ending list of questions. Neither of us speaks now. The silence is heavy, the unspoken words and memories from last night floating like an invisible, choking mist. Something broke between us last night. I don't know how to repair it. Or if I want to repair it. I catch Tristan looking at me a couple times, but he looks away when I meet his eyes.

I steal glances at him too. His capable arms fortify the fence, the muscles on them flexing with effort. I used to look at his strong, defined body with admiration—thinking how well he can protect us.

Now my thoughts are far from being so innocent. All I can think of is how those same arms enveloped me last night, holding me against him, caressing me with a fervor I've never experienced before. As his lips move, gasping for air—the hot, humid air that's never enough to satiate our need for fresh air—our kiss flashes right before my eyes. His lips over mine, coaxing me, setting me ablaze. His tongue and its desperate dance with mine.

It was passionate.

Raw.

Impossible to forget.

But over the next few days I try to do the impossible. Cold silence hangs between us as we plant spine plants in front of fence, building our little fort. Tristan goes back to sleeping in the cockpit at night. I don't do anything to stop him, telling myself it's for the best, convincing myself he won't have nightmares again. He doesn't need me anymore.

All of which proves to be a lie. Maybe it's because I'm now intimately aware of his nightmares, but in addition to hearing him thrash around in his sleep, I make out the words he mumbles, despite the closed door. I break down after three nights and go to him in the cockpit. I wake him up, his horror-filled eyes finding their focus and peace when he sees me. He opens his mouth, but I put my thumb on it, shaking my head. I lead him to the cabin, on my seat. He puts his head on my chest, entwining his fingers with mine, his breath rapid at first, then more shallow until he falls in a restful sleep.

Chapter 22

Aimee

The next afternoon, I head straight to the shower, exhausted after a trip to check the water level at the bottom of the hill. The water receded some more, and Tristan predicts we should be able to leave this place in about one month. One month! After having spent almost three months here, that shouldn't seem like such a long time. But with the threat of two or more jaguars looming over us, it seems like an eternity. Hopefully the spine bushes we planted around the outside of the fence will keep them away. I spend an inordinate amount of time in the shower, rubbing my skin, cleaning myself. I ran too close to one of the spine bushes near the entrance and scratched my right shoulder. The spines must contain some kind of coloring sap, because my scratch is a jet black that doesn't go away no matter how hard I rub it. Hopefully it will go away in a few days. I'm almost done showering when I hear

Tristan's voice.

"Aimee, get inside the plane. Now." I don't move, paralyzed by fear, clutching the dress I was about to put on. A hundred different scenarios play in my head as I try to imagine what prompted Tristan to sound so desperate. "Aimee."

This time I do move. Fast. I sling the dress over my head and jump out of the shower. Instead of getting inside the plane, I grab my bow and a few arrows. I look around for my spear, but don't find it anywhere. Instead, I find Tristan, his bow and arrow in his hands, ready to shoot. He's standing with his back to me, in front of a giant hole in the fence. A fresh one.

So much for the spines protecting us. Tristan has his arrow pointed at the hole, as if he's expecting something to burst through it any minute. I have a hunch I know what.

"The jaguar who made that hole is still around?" I ask.

"I told you to get inside the plane," Tristan hisses.

"Well, I didn't. Deal with it." I point my arrow at the hole as well, stepping next to Tristan. "Don't try to argue with me, just tell me what's going on. What's the plan?"

My throat constricts as I stare at the hole, but I manage not to panic.

"I haven't been able to formulate a plan beyond killing him on sight."

"Is it just one jaguar?"

Tristan pauses for a few beats, then nods. "Smear your arrow tips with poison." I do as he says, grateful that we decided to tie the pouches with poison on the bow yesterday.

"Have you seen my spear?" I ask, feeling unprotected with just the bow and the arrows, since my aim is still far from being of any use.

"It's propped against our wood supply."

I slowly back up, not taking my eyes off Tristan. He is fixed on the hole, his grasp on the bow firm, ready to release the arrow. His shoulders hunch forward; his white shirt is soaked to his skin. I've never seen him so tense.

When I get to the wood shelter I peel my gaze off him, bending to pick up my spear.

"Aimee, if you care about me at all, get inside that damn plane. Now." The jaguar has come into view at last. Tristan's words carry a thinly veiled panic that turns me into stone. I can't take refuge in the plane, even though I fear what we're about to face.

More powerful than that is the fear of losing him. I can't hide inside the plane *precisely* because I care about him. Why did it take this to realize just how much? The feeling is so clear, so natural, it's like it has always been there. But I've subdued it so fiercely that it strikes back with an intensity that hurts.

Most powerful than everything, though, is the need to protect him. From my crouched position, I see the dreaded orange and black fur of a jaguar through the hole in the fence. I grip my spear in one hand, my bow in the other one. I bounce to my feet with a grating noise, a branch snapping beneath my feet. Maybe if it hadn't, Tristan wouldn't have looked my way, and the disaster would have been averted.

But it did snap.

Tristan's head turns to me, and his eyes leave the hole for a fraction of a second. But a fraction of a second is all it takes for the hellish nightmare to begin.

No words come out of his open mouth. Instead, a scream splinters the air. Piercing and horrifying. Like a lightning bolt, it courses through me, paralyzing me, sucking every wisp of air from my lungs. The next seconds are excruciating. They pass too fast for me to be able to react, but seem long enough for me to take in every gory detail. I see Tristan's bow fly out of his hand as he lands on his back, muddy water splashing in every direction. When he raises his left hand over his head in a defensive move, I see my worst fear soaking through his shirt, one blotch of blood at a time. My knees buckle. I won't be able to reach him in time to spear the jaguar preparing to attack him. Judging by its size it is a cub, not the mother. But the cub is large enough to do permanent damage. Large enough to be deadly. I drop my spear, take one of the arrows, and place it in my bow. My hands tremble. I'm terrified of releasing the arrow. But I do. And it misses.

I let out a huge breath though, because the arrow isn't totally useless. It distracted the jaguar. For one tiny moment; then it turns its attention toward Tristan again. A blink of an eye later, Tristan yelps with pain, both his arms crossed in front of him. More red dots appear on the white sleeves. But the worst is yet to come, because the beast used only its claws to attack until now, not its fangs. My heart in my throat, I release another arrow. I let out a primal, horrifying sound. The arrow almost hits Tristan. And it's poisoned. If one single arrow hits him—

The recognition pumps life in my limp legs. I drop the bow and pick up my spear again. And then I dart toward them, passing by Tristan's bow. I don't have a plan other than spearing the beast. I don't know if that'll help much or not. I'll throw myself between them if need be. All I care about is distracting the beast. When I'm less than a foot away from them, I draw in a sharp breath and lunge forward with all my weight, spearing the jaguar in one side. It jerks back, the brusque movement unbalancing me. I fall flat on my face in the mud, a numbing pain spreading over the side of my face. I turn around at the sound of a riveting grunt behind me. Tristan's on his feet, clutching his arrows. I don't understand what he's doing, or why he's walking backward, until I see the bow on the ground. He's trying to reach the bow. But he won't make it in time. He won't. The jaguar is already poised to attack. One leap forward and Tristan will be beneath him. Beyond saving. I try to push myself up, and hurt my palm on a pointy stone.

That's when it hits me.

Stones.

The sound of my heart slamming against my ribcage pounds in my ears as I frantically scratch to remove the half-buried stone from the earth. It's huge. That's good. It will do some damage. I hurt my fingers in the process of digging the stone out. I throw it in the direction of the animal with both hands, aiming for its head, but it hits his side, where my spear wounded him earlier. The cat roars in confusion, his head snapping in my direction. His predatory gaze lands on me. Pain pierces my chest, stopping any air from coming in. Every inch of my clammy skin twitches. My mind is too clenched by fear to formulate a plan. My body seems to have a will of its own and starts crawling backward. But the beast is advancing toward me already. I can't outrun it. I can't beat it. I close my eyes, crossing my arms in front of me as Tristan did earlier. I grind my teeth, my body shaking like a leaf. I wait for the attack, bracing myself for excruciating pain. When a howl resounds, I'm surprised it doesn't come from my own lips. Still shaking, I open my eyes. Through my crossed arms I see the animal howling, still heading my way, though its steps are slower. An arrow is sticking out of the side of its neck. When the second arrow pierces him, the animal sways, collapsing a few inches from my feet. Its passing isn't as quick as the small animals Tristan tested the arrows on, but no more than a few seconds go by before the beast dies.

I become aware of pain in every part of my body. On the side of my face where I hit the ground when I fell, in my fingers from digging for the stone. But I couldn't care less. All I care about is that Tristan is alive and walking. His sleeves have quite a few blood stains, but somehow there aren't as many as I imagined earlier. He doesn't seem hurt. He's smeared with mud, just like me.

He kneels next to me. Unable to say anything, I sling my arms around him, tears streaming down my cheeks as I press my ear against the soaked fabric on his chest.

"Aimee, are you hurt?" Tristan murmurs in my ear. Apprehension colors his voice.

"No. But you are."

Through the shredded sleeves of his shirt I can

see his skin and it sickens me. "Let me take your shirt off," I say with a trembling voice.

"Let's get away from this first," he says, motioning toward the dead jaguar cub. Fear courses through me as I realize that what we just did will bring the fury of the jaguar mother upon us. I'm certain there will be a retaliation. I dearly hope she does not have any other cubs, because I don't know how we will defend ourselves if she does.

"What are we going to do with it?" I ask.

"I'll take care of it later."

I make Tristan sit on the airstairs, and I remove his shirt, careful not to hurt him. When I see his arms, every muscle in my body relaxes a notch. His scratches are not as deep as I thought, though they run along both his arms, and certainly need cleaning and disinfecting. I run inside the plane and rip a strip of fabric from my wedding dress, then grab the first aid kit. My diamond rings slips off my finger, falling with a hollow sound on the floor next to my suitcase. In my haste to get back to Tristan, I don't even think of stopping to retrieve it.

Outside, I dip the fabric in water, then run it along his arms, cleaning the long scratches. Though the scratches aren't deep, blood trickles from a few of them. I start shaking, the sight of blood mingling with the white of the fabric too much for me to bear. No matter how much I grit my teeth and bite my lips, I can't stop fresh tears from rolling down my cheeks.

"Aimee," Tristan says tenderly, tilting my chin to meet his gaze, "it doesn't hurt that bad, I promise."

"I don't..." I take a deep breath. I need to pull myself together. But my voice is undependable when I continue. "I was so afraid something would happen to you."

I realize I can't talk about this. At least not right now. The terror is still too fresh, the fear of losing him still has an iron grip on me.

He takes my bloody fingers in his palms, cleaning them with water, just as I did with his arms. Then he bends forward, kissing my hands, in a gesture so tender, so pure, that I'd like nothing better than to steal this moment and encase it in a glass bubble, a haven safe from the forest. Safe from the world and its judgement. Safe from my own judgement. Tristan stays like this for a few seconds, then pulls me in a tight hug, his forehead buried in my hair, his lips touching my neck. "I've never been more afraid of anything than I was of losing you today, Aimee." His voice trembles, yet the words tumble out fast, as if he's afraid I will stop him. "All I could think of was you'd be taken away from me before I got to tell you how much you mean to me."

"I know," I whisper, pulling him up, resting my forehead against his. "I know. I—" I stop when I notice blood trickling again from the scratches on his arms. "I have to bandage your arms. On second thought, take a shower and wash all the mud away. I'll bandage your arms afterward."

Tristan doesn't question me, but his eyes probe me with worry, which is ridiculous, because I am fine.

I stay just outside the shower while he's inside, unable to bring myself to move from this spot, shaken by the irrational fear that something may happen to him if I stray too far, that something will take him away from me. He walks out wearing the fresh pair of pants I put there for him earlier. He didn't put on the shirt I also put there. He looks as strong as ever, as long as I keep my eyes away from his arms and on his steel chest and broad shoulders. But then blood trickles from one of his scratches again, and all my fears are back. I take the bandages, rubbing alcohol, and what's left of the antibiotic cream out of the first aid kit when we return to the airstairs.

"No, don't use the antibiotic cream," Tristan says.

"Why? The scratches can become infected."

"We shouldn't waste it."

"Waste it? Tristan, your arms need it."

"Maybe we'll need it more later. We could get attacked again, and if you get hurt..." He drops his eyes to his hands, his tone apologetic.

Always thinking of me first. Always.

"Let me be the one who worries about you for once, okay?" I say. "Just let me apply it. Please. You need it."

I sense that he'd like to argue further, but I shake my head and he gives in, allowing me to take care of him. After I'm done bandaging his arms I tell him, "Go inside the plane and rest. It's almost dark anyway. I'll take a shower and then come inside."

"No, I'll wait for you here," he says. "Just in case. I want to keep an eye out."

I nod, understanding his apprehension. I felt the same before.

Showering usually calms me, and I never hurry the process, but now I can't wait to get out. Being separated from Tristan, even if he's just a few feet away, causes me to shudder with fear that something might happen to him.

When I get out, Tristan takes my hand, leading me inside the plane. The warmth of his palm spreads through me, making my nerve endings tingle. I allow myself to give in to the sense of security he brings to everything

I don't pull my hand away. I don't ever want to pull it away.

Chapter 23

Aimee

When we enter the plane, Tristan hovers in front of the door to the cockpit.

"Sleep next to me tonight, Tristan."

Turning toward me he asks, "Are you sure?"

"Yes." I run my hand from one shoulder blade to the other, and I feel goose bumps forming on his skin. "Tonight. Every night."

I don't know if he was expecting us to sleep separately, but I wedge myself next to him. After what happened today, nothing feels close enough. I cocoon myself against him, resting my head on his shoulder. "I feel fine. Relax, Aimee."

I can't. The jaguar's growl still rings in my ears. It brings back the paralyzing fear of losing Tristan. I inch closer to him, the warmth of his naked torso doing wonders for my stiff posture. He presses his fingers on the back of my neck, and I moan as some of the tension built up inside releases. Tristan's fingers freeze on my neck.

"Aimee..."

My name on his lips undoes me again. It awakens something dangerous inside me. He's said it before, but now it sounds different. I turn my head so I can look him in the eyes. He shifts his arm under my head, his fingers reaching to stroke my cheek. He's trapped me in his half embrace, and I don't want him to let go. Here, in the safety of his arms, I find the strength to talk about the fear of losing him.

"I was so scared, you have no idea."

"I do," he says softly. "After I came back from Afghanistan, I was certain I would never fear anything again. But now I'm afraid every time I see a new hole in the fence, terrified that something might happen to you. I never dared to hope you felt that way too."

My breath hitches, but I don't pull away. My relief is so overwhelming I don't want to separate from him even one inch. So I don't. Not even when he leans in closer. His lips feather mine with a gentle touch, and a slight shudder shakes me. He's expecting me to back out. I do no such thing. Instead, I beckon him to kiss me, and he does. His full lips coax mine, their softness filling me with warmth. And igniting something inside me I won't have the power to stop.

I don't want it to stop anymore. This tenderness surprises me. It's so different from our first kiss. Tristan moves slightly, taking his arm from underneath my head and pushing me into the chair as his kiss becomes more urgent. I cradle his head with my arms, forcing him to kiss me even deeper. I'm rewarded with a groan. With one swift move, he pulls me underneath him. His expansive chest pushes against my breasts, and a deep throb pulses low in my body. Desire takes a life of its own when he slams his hips against mine, and I feel his need for me—his hard length strained by the fabric of his pants. In a haze, he frees me of the straps on my shoulders and pushes my dress down to my hips, revealing my breasts. His lips dart to my neck, suckling their way to my collarbone and then to my breasts, leaving a trail of fire in their wake that burns away any ounce of control I still have.

"Tristan," I gasp, my fingers digging in his back, craving for more. I want him to kiss me again, yet I don't want his mouth to stop the sweet torture on my breasts. Need sears through me, and I buck my hips in an involuntary move, pressing hard against him. His hand shoots under my dress, up my thighs, and he begins to remove my underwear. I still. He must sense my hesitation, because his hand stops. His fingers brush my inner thigh so closely to my intimate spot my need turns into delirious craving.

"You want me to stop?" he asks in a low growl against my neck. I try to form words, but I'm unable to, the pulsing desire surging through every nerve ending. In response, I unzip his pants. I push them down with his underwear as he pushes down my dress and panties.

"You're so beautiful," he says in a breathy voice. In the moonlight, I see his heavy-lidded eyes raking over my naked body. I'm shaking with consuming need. His eyes meet mine, and my need is mirrored in his dark gaze. He cups my backside greedily with one hand and sinks into my core with abandon.

"Aimeeeeeeeeeee," he grits in the curve of my

neck, the feral sound spearing through me.

His hands are everywhere. Grazing the skin on my thighs, cupping my breasts. His passion pushes me to the edge, until I'm brazen enough to let out without restraint the proof of my own passion. I buckle my hips with urgency, swooping my lips over his neck, digging my nails in his chest as he drives into me with more and more urgency, spurring tremors so intense, I feel like I will splinter apart. I've never been so desperate for release. But I've also never made love like this before. My inner flesh clenches around his hard length, and, as he feasts on my body, I revel in pleasure, discovering I can cause so much desire. I spiral into explosive bliss with an intense cry that wracks my body. I feel him pull out, and rest confused for a moment when he empties his own relief away from me, then remember we had no protection.

Afterward, he slumps next to me, burying his head in my neck, exhaling hot breaths over me. He puts one of his arms around me. I swallow hard and take a better look at his arm.

"Tristan, your arm is bleeding." Little red blotches have made their appearance on the stark white bandage.

"It's nothing. I strained the arm a little too much."

"Let me look at it." I try to get in a sitting position, but he holds me.

"No, please. I just want to hold you like this," he murmurs in my ear.

"I'm not going anywhere." I give in to his plea. I snuggle up with him, closing my eyes, tracing my fingers on his back, feeling at peace with myself for once. When Tristan falls asleep, I stare at the night outside the window, waiting for the guilt to overcome me.

It doesn't.

I remember the burdensome guilt I felt over having feelings for Tristan. I remember how suffocating it weighed on me after we kissed. I try to recall the intensity of it all, but I can't.

Compared to the horrible fear I experienced today, and the devastating possibility of losing Tristan, nothing feels as intense. Or as important. Not the guilt. And nothing that came before we crashed here. That's how I know I made the right decision by giving myself to him tonight, and there is no going back. Tristan slipped into my soul the way mist travels in the forest after the rain: unseen, unstoppable, and ubiquitous. Our feelings resemble the mist in a way, too. When you're surrounded by the mist you don't see it clearly, though you feel it in the thickness of the air. You know it's there, but you can't touch it or know for sure if it is real. But if you take a step back, or look at it from above, it's as clear as if it were snow.

Mist perhaps isn't the best comparison, because it disappears after a while, though it returns with every rain. My feelings for him are not going to disappear.

Smiling, I climb out of the chair, careful not to wake him up, and walk to the back of the plane. In the darkness, I grope the floor where I lost my ring today, until I find it. I clasp my fingers around the cold metal. The diamond scratching my palm used to embody almost everything for me. Hope, love, happiness. And lately, guilt.

But as I unzip an outer pocket of my suitcase

and drop the ring inside it, an exhilarating sense of freedom overtakes me. A twinge of guilt remains, of course, because no matter how I put it, I'm betraying the man who once meant a lot to me, but whom I can now think of as nothing more than my best friend. That in itself is a betrayal. But, I won't cling to the feeling of remorse any longer.

Being on the brink of losing everything had the remarkable power of setting me free.

I've decided what I will tell Chris and how I will set things right if I ever see him again. After today's events, the probability of that happening seem slim. Until now, marching through the forest after the water level sunk, back to civilization, seemed like a certainty. A plan that wasn't without its faults, but a plan. We just had to wait for the right time, and we'd go home. I believed we would get there. Even lighting up the signal fire every day... I've been doing it in the hope that maybe we'd get lucky and get rescued after all. That possibly a stray plane would fly above this region and see our signal. In any case, I never doubted we would get home, eventually, either by a plane or going back on foot. Today, I had a taste of how real the possibility of not making it out of the jungle is.

The nightmares disturbing my sleep tonight are my own. In them, the jaguar isn't dead. Instead, it rips Tristan's flesh apart while all the arrows I shoot miss their target.

Chapter 24

Aimee

The bow vibrates in my hands as I release arrow after arrow. I don't know how long I have been shooting, and I don't care. I won't stop until every damn arrow hits the target. Judging by the pile of arrows huddled at the roots of the tree—the proof of my ineptitude—I'll be at it a long time. My fingers don't even hurt anymore, though they felt as if they were on fire at some point. Now they're numb.

When I woke up this morning, the bloody bandage on Tristan's arm and the realization of how close the beast came to killing him overwhelmed me again.

I left him asleep and came outside, trying to clear my head. Seeing the dead jaguar's body had the opposite effect, and I ended up with the bow between my fingers. I shoot again and again, tears of desperation rolling down my cheeks. Shoot. Miss. Shoot. Miss. Shoot. Hit.

"Aimee." Tristan's voice sounds desperate, if distant. "Aimee, stop."

But I don't stop. I can't. Tristan grips both my wrists, forcing me to stop. He steps in front of me. "Aimee, *what* are you doing?"

"I don't know," I whisper. The events of yesterday afternoon play in my mind like a bad movie. The jaguar jumping forward. Tristan falling backward. My utter ineptitude to shoot the animal. The magnitude of it all hits me in one giant wave and my knees tremble. All I manage to blabber before I burst into an ugly cry is, "I don't want you to die because of my incompetency."

"I won't—Aimee, you are hurting yourself. Let the bow go." When I don't react he raises his voice, desperation piercing it. "Aimee."

He unclenches my fingers from the bow, taking it away. That's when I see my fingers. They're worse than yesterday. The skin is shredded where they touched the bow.

"I am so sorry," I say through sobs.

"Shhh, you're having a meltdown."

Tristan drops the bow, putting an arm around my waist, patting me on the back. "Calm down, Aimee. I'm all right. It barely hurts anymore."

I sob even harder. "But you could have died. I could have lost you."

"Please don't say that." His voice is soothing, and I find myself relaxing in his tender embrace. "Let's go inside the plane and take care of your fingers."

"No, I'm fine." Ashamed of my meltdown, I try to pull myself together. "We have lots to do and I—"

Tristan scoops me up in his injured arms, but I don't protest or ask him to put me down. I rest my head on his shoulder, enjoying the rhythmic beat of his heart. Somehow, it has the power to drive away any thought. When he puts me down in my seat, I draw my knees up to my chest, feeling cold without his arms on me.

"I'll be back in a sec," he says.

He brings the bottle of alcohol and a strip from my wedding dress then kneels in front of me, tending to my callused fingers. I try to be brave, like he was yesterday, but I start whimpering as soon as the cloth touches my skin.

"Aimee, what did you feel last night?" His voice has a strained quality to it, as if he's bracing himself for my answer.

I don't answer, considering my words for a long time. Too long.

He begins to turn away, but I grip his wrist and his head snaps back toward me. He caresses my cheek with the back of his fingers, sending tendrils of sparks through me. "I don't regret what happened between us, Tristan."

He kisses my forehead, murmuring, "It's the most beautiful thing that's happened to me."

Something flutters in my chest at his words. They're so pure, so heartfelt that I almost liquefy. "Let me change the bandage on your arm," I say.

"I've looked at it this morning. It's fine, no need to change it. We have to be careful not to waste the bandages."

I run my fingers over his bandaged arm, as if that would help me find out if he's telling the truth. He doesn't wince at my touch, so he's not in pain. All of a sudden he grabs my wrist, looking down at my fingers.

"You're not wearing your ring."

"No... I don't feel the need to wear it anymore."

He raises his eyes to mine. Slowly—as if he doesn't dare to believe what I said.

"Do you mean that?" he asks in a low voice.

I nod, not quite able to say the words out loud. But there's no sense denying this. There are many things you can hide in the rainforest. But not lies. Or love.

I lean in and kiss him.

Chapter 25

Aimee

His lips part in surprise, but then his mouth settles over mine in a soft kiss. Before long, the heat that only he can stir to life starts building inside me. I deepen the kiss with urgency, both my hands darting at the crook of his neck.

"Slow down, Aimee," he says, gasping for breath, "why are you in so much of a rush?"

I bite my lip, ashamed. "I thought you liked it this way."

"I love it." He pushes a strand of hair behind my ear. "But I don't want to rush this today. Last night, I didn't have enough self-restraint to give myself to you and make love to you the way you deserve."

I frown in confusion. "And which way is that?"

"Completely."

My breath stumbles as I climb in his lap, hitching my legs around his waist. Tristan unbuttons my shirt with exquisite slowness, placing a kiss on my skin after he pops each button open. I revel in the feeling; the brush of his lips on my skin sending hot and cold shivers down my spine, prompting a painful ache deep down in my body.

"I meant to ask you, what's this?" He points to the scratch on my shoulder. The one I got by running into the spine bush outside the fence at the entrance. The scratch is just as black as it was when I got it.

"Yesterday I scratched myself with some of those spines I planted near the entrance. The black doesn't wash off. Will it be permanent?"

"I doubt it." He resumes taking off my shirt. My job is easier, since he has no shirt on. I take in the rippled muscles of his stomach, the strong, hard-as-steel shoulders, and after I yank down his pants, I delight in his muscled legs. He lays me on my back, stripping me and then covering my body in kisses.

"I want to memorize every single part of your body," he says in a breathy voice as he feasts on my inner thighs and then the valley between my breasts. Each kiss fuels the passion brewing between my thighs, pushing me further down the slope of consuming need.

When I can't tolerate the ache anymore, I pull him to me, kissing him, and rocking my hips against his. He plunges inside me, filling me, ripping whimper after whimper out of me. His mouth dusts my arms, calling my name in deep, guttural sounds that unhinge me. He increases the pace of his moves, thrusting so deep my thighs wobble. Eagerness swirls up inside me as wave after wave of pleasure engulf me, my body surging forward when my release shatters me.

We lie in each other's arms for a long time afterward. I trace my fingers along the expanse of his chest while he plays with my hair.

"You didn't sleep well last night," Tristan says.

"I had bad dreams. But you didn't have any."

"No. They tend to stay away when I'm with you. I was searching for peace in my nightmares. But when I'm with you, I don't have to search for anything. I already have everything. I feel whole." I catch my breath as he continues. "I need you in a way I never thought I could need anything. It's like air. You don't notice how much you need it until you don't have it. I love you, Aimee. For being selfless and giving me your strength. For giving me the things I never knew I needed. If there's something I learned in war, it's that no one is unimportant. Every person means the world to someone. That makes us vulnerable, but it also makes life a gift. I had no one who could give me that gift. Now I do."

When you find the person who sees you clearer than you see yourself, you know you've found true love. "I love you too," I whisper.

"Can I tell you something very selfish?" he asks.

"Can't wait to hear it."

"A small part of me wishes we could stay here forever."

"How can you say that?" I snap my head up, raising my eyebrows.

He takes a deep breath, cupping my cheek with his hand, his thumb caressing my lips. "Because I've found something here I've never had before. Hope. You gave it to me. And I have you here. You're more than I've ever had, and more than I'll ever wish for."

He stops, as if what he planned to say next is too painful to express. But I don't pull my eyes away from him. "If we go back, things will be like they were before... and I can't bear losing you."

"Nothing will be the same as before," I say, sitting up, affronted. "You think I'll go back to Chris? Marry him? Of course I won't." His eyes search me, doubt reflected in them. "You're not the only one who found hope here, Tristan." He pulls me into a long, heartfelt kiss and doesn't let go until my stomach growls, reminding both of us that my meltdown and our lovemaking kept us away from food.

"We'd better go search for some fruit," I say, pushing him away. "Unless you can shoot something with your hurt arms."

"I might."

As we both dress I say, "I still want us to be found. Even if it means facing Chris and telling him everything."

"How do you imagine he'll take it?" he asks in a clipped tone.

"He'll forgive us." Chris has always been that kind of person. Which makes hurting him so much crueller. "I am not sure if I was truly in love with him," I whisper, voicing the doubts that have plagued me since I first acknowledged Tristan's effect on me. "I cared about him a lot. I still do. But... what I feel for you is so intense, so different... I've never felt that way about him." I never had with him the kind of connection I have with Tristan, one that runs so deep, it seems to run through my veins. Chris didn't understand me in that profound way Tristan does, even when I thoroughly explained things to him, like how I feel about my parents. Tristan understands with just a few words, and sometimes, with no words at all.

Tristan's expression brightens and I realize this is something that has weighed on him a lot.

"That was a common theme among the employees at the Moore's mansion," he says as we exit the plane.

"What was?"

"That the two of you seemed more like best friends; you lacked a spark."

I groan. "How would you know what the employees at the mansion said? You work for Chris, not his parents."

He raises an eyebrow. "I drove you to the mansion on a number of occasions, and waited for you there until you were ready to go. That gave Maggie and the rest of the staff plenty of time to fill me in on... things."

"People talked about us?"

"Yeah... Maggie said she always thought of you as siblings, didn't expect the two of you to be a couple."

"I wish Maggie had told me that." Many people told me that, but Maggie is someone I listen to, having raised Chris and me. I wonder if she ever told Chris. I wonder if he had second thoughts about us when his friends told him what my friends told me: that we seem to love each other like a brother and sister. And most of all I wonder if, in the months I've been gone, he may have found someone else.

I pray that he did.

"Plenty of birds flying around." I point to the sky as Tristan flexes the string of the bow, indicating that he can shoot. Shy sunrays garland the trees, making the green appear so vivid it ricochets from the shiny texture. Tatters of light hang on the lower branches, guiding our steps as we venture outside. "Won't have to wait long for our meal. Use your perfect aim on one of those unsuspecting birds, and then while I cook it, you can get rid of the jaguar body."

Tristan grins, looking up at the multitude of birds. "Guess we're lucky today."

Chapter 26

Aimee

But the last of our luck evaporates less than two weeks later. Weeks in which we fall blissfully into each other's arms every night. I love him with a scintillating intensity that grows every day. I never knew love could be like this. But I suppose this only happens when you connect at a level so deep and powerful it casts everything before it into meaninglessness. A connection built with spoken and unspoken words alike.

During these weeks, we fight the jungle during daylight. It seems more determined than ever to defeat us. Fresh holes appear in the fence every day, and our water baskets and wood supply are trashed each night—all signs the female jaguar has more than the one cub we killed. Judging by the paw prints, she has three others. There is a light at the end of the tunnel, though. The water has receded to a level where we can almost walk through it, and Tristan has started making serious plans about our trip into the wild in search of civilization. We stop our daily poem exchange. Survival requires our full attention. Every free minute we brainstorm about potential dangers on the trip back, and what we can do to prepare for them. We're practicing building basic shelters. We've been lucky with the plane, but when we leave, we'll have to build every night a shelter strong enough to keep us safe from beasts. We also try to collect as much animal fat as we can. Torches will be indispensable out there. At the same time, we double our efforts to secure the fence, and even set poison food traps for the jaguars, but they are too smart to touch them. We just need to fend them off for another few weeks, then we'll be ready to go.

However, our downfall doesn't come, as we feared, from the jaguars.

"You haven't eaten anything," I exclaim after I finish devouring my bird leg and two roots. I was starving today, and my portion hasn't done much to satisfy my hunger. I lean back, propping my elbows on the rough bark of the trunk that serves as our eating place. My muscles are sore from building shelter after shelter today. We've set a new record, building the simplest shelter in about ten minutes. It's an emergency shelter in case it rains unexpectedly. Tristan hasn't touched his food at all. He's staring at it as if the mere sight makes him sick.

"No, I'm not hungry."

"But we haven't eaten all day. You need your strength."

"I don't feel like eating. I guess I'm just exhausted. You can have my portion, you're still hungry."

He pushes his leaf plate in my direction. I catch his hand, and squeeze it. It feels cold and weak, and that scares me. "Go to sleep. I'll be next to you in a minute. You'll get better tomorrow." I watch him drag himself up the airstairs and inside the plane. I'm not hungry anymore.

He doesn't get better. First thing in the morning, he throws up. His body has a slight tremor to it as I help him sit on the steps. He's covered in cold sweat.

"Can it be from something you ate the day before yesterday? No, it can't be. We've been eating the same food."

"I don't know." He presses his palms on the sides of his head, his elbows resting on his knees. "I was throwing up yesterday, too."

"What?" I ask, alarmed. "When? Why didn't you tell me?"

"I didn't want to worry you."

I hug him to my chest, tasting bile at the back of my throat. This close, I feel like every tremor of his is mine, and they fill me with a debilitating fear.

"What do you think it is?"

"Some kind of disease. Maybe from mosquitoes, maybe from some kind of bacteria in the food or water."

"That can't be," I say, almost like a plea. "Why I am not sick then?"

"Our immune systems aren't identical. Even if what we eat and drink is."

Something inside me crumbles—with the speed of the lightning. And its intensity too. But I force my voice to stay steady when I say, "Stay inside today and rest, okay?" He doesn't even attempt to argue;

that worries me like nothing else. The moment he's out of sight, tears spill down my cheeks. This can't be happening. Not now. Not when we're so close to leaving this place. Not when we're so close to being safe. Though I have a million things to do, I go inside every half hour to help him drink water and check on him. He's sleeping most of the time, his body temperature higher every time I put my hand to his forehead. As the sun is about to set I grill some roots. When I walk inside the plane to take some to Tristan, he's gone.

I blink, spinning around, taking in every inch of the cabin. The muscles in my legs tighten as I make my way to the cockpit. He isn't there, either. I stand on the edge of the door, gripping the edges, my knuckles white. I was less than ten feet away from the bottom of the airstairs. I should have heard him leave. But did he leave? His pocketknife, bow, and arrows are still propped on the airstairs, where they've been the whole day, which means he's unarmed. The thought of him wandering in the rainforest without anything to defend himself gives me chest pains. I stand on my toes, scanning the space outside the fence. Not very far from the makeshift gate of the fence, I see Tristan, crawling more than walking. Stumbling. I run toward him, picking up my own bow and arrows in the process.

When I reach him I stand in front of him, blocking his way. "Tristan, what are you doing?"

His skin pale and sweaty, he answers, "I need to stay away from you. You might get sick too."

"No, I won't."

His unfocused gaze and the creases of confusion on his forehead tell me he isn't thinking clearly. As

I watch him I remember a particularly worrisome piece of information Chris once shared: some animals hide to be alone when they are about to die.

"Tristan, please stop arguing with me." My voice shakes. "Let me take you back to the plane."

"No, you don't understand. The mosquitoes... I may have malaria, or yellow fever. I could give what I have to you too," he mumbles. His knees buckle and I put his arm over my shoulders, grabbing him by the waist to support him. He tries to fight me off, but he's too weak.

"You're not being reasonable. Those are diseases that are transmitted by mosquito bites only." When I put my hand on his forehead I can see why he isn't being reasonable. His skin burns with a fever so high I'm certain his mind must be foggy. Fever is a symptom of a truckload of tropical diseases. Which one does he have and what is the mortality rate?

"Let's walk back; come on." He's so weak he can't fight, and starts putting one foot in front of the other. There are maybe a hundred feet until the plane, but we're going so slow, it'll take us half an hour to get there. I keep my ears tuned for danger, clutching my bow for dear life. I feel vulnerable now, even though I'm better with the bow than I've ever been. If something attacks us now, I can't react fast enough. There's no way I can protect Tristan, who seems to be on the verge of collapse. Those words play in my mind again and again. *Mortality rate*. I shake my head, tightening my grasp on the bow. I need to get him to safety first, and then I'll worry about the mortality rate.

I'm drenched in sweat by the time I lay Tristan

on his seat in the plane. Tristan's fever has soaked through his shirt so I help him change into a new one. I light a torch with some shreds of my wedding dress and go outside for a basket of water. I intend to use it for compresses to bring down his fever, but since the water isn't cold... What is effective against tropical diseases? I don't even know which one he's got, so I focus on what I do know. He has a fever. He needs to keep hydrated. I breathe in, refusing to cry.

When I'm back inside, I secure the torch and soak one of my shirts in water, then charge toward Tristan.

I freeze in my steps when I see him. He's curled in a fetal position, shaking, his teeth chattering, his eyes unfocused. I drop the shirt, rushing to him, kneeling by his side. He's mumbling something I can't make out, so I put my ear as close to his lips as possible. I realize I can't understand what he's saying because my heart is thumping in my ears. *Pull yourself together Aimee; you can't help him if you lose it. Come on.*

But when he interlaces his burning fingers with mine, I do lose it, and the tears I've been holding back start rolling down my cheeks. I wipe them away. I don't want him to see me crying.

"Cold," he says through his chattering teeth. His eyes are unfocused.

"You're cold, of course." I slap my forehead. "That's why you're shaking. I'll bring you blankets." I try to untangle his fingers from mine, but he doesn't let go. "Tristan, I'll get some blankets. I'll be back in a second." My voice undependable, I continue, "You have to let go of my fingers, my love. Please."

At the word love, he focuses his eyes on me for

a second before sliding away again. He lets go of my hand. I bring two blankets and throw them over him. He's shaking just as much as before.

"Cold," he mutters. "So cold."

"There are no more blankets, Tristan." My voice crackles and I realize he's not hearing me, or acknowledging me. I bring the basket of water next to him, making him drink and putting compresses on his forehead. They don't help at all. His skin gets hotter by the minute while his trembling worsens, repeating the word *cold* every few minutes. I cradle his head with my arms, perching myself on top of him under the blankets, hoping some of my body heat will seep into his.

To my astonishment, his eyes fly wide open. "You shouldn't be this close to me. You'll get sick..."

"Shh... I won't. Trust me on this, please."

"You can make it fine on your own. You can feed yourself and make fires." It takes all his strength to speak. "You're strong and brave. You can make it through the forest on your own."

"Don't talk like this, please. You'll be all right, you'll see."

"Aimee," his voice holds such urgency, horror trickles in my veins. "I might not wake up tomorrow."

"I don't... No, you'll—"

"You have to accept that."

I lean in to kiss him, tears pouring down my cheeks. He refuses to open his lips, still afraid of making me sick. "If you don't wake up tomorrow morning, I don't want to wake up either," I whisper. He wraps his arms around me. I never want him to let go. He gives in to my kiss at last, and I coax his fever-cracked lips open with mine, caressing his tongue tenderly.

"You don't need me to survive," he says.

"You're right. I don't need you to survive. I need you to live." I bury my head in the crook of his neck, grateful to be feeling his pulse against my cheek.

"You don't need anyone. You're like a star, Aimee. Stars shine from within. They don't need anything else."

This talk of stars means that his delirium is bad. I fist his shirt with trembling hands, as if this will help me keep him from sliding into a world where I can't reach him.

"I'm not a star," I whisper. "I'm a satellite rotating around you. You're the star. I need your light to shine."

"I could say the same."

"Let's agree that we are each other's star, then," I say.

"You can only discover your own light in the darkness."

I've been in the darkness. There is no light to be found in it. But I don't argue with him. Light doesn't come from darkness, but from something else... from kindness and understanding, the kind he showed me. In sharing his pain, he took mine away. In sharing his nightmares, he showed me just how endless the darkness can seem. By letting me chase away his nightmares, we both learned how to find light. Together.

I wish I could find words to tell him how much he means to me. But I've never been good with words, and if I try to talk, I might end up speaking of stars, just like he has. But I'm not the one who is delirious, though the pain and fear of losing him may have spurred a delirium of their own.

I just say, "I love you, Tristan," and kiss him anew.

"You'll be all right. You'll do your best. Promise me," he whispers between kisses, tightening his hug even more. He still wants to protect me, like always, despite the fact that death is knocking at his door. He can't protect me from the one thing I fear most: his death. I want to tell him I won't be all right, that I can't be all right in a world where he is no more. But when we stop kissing, his eyes are burning with an urgency that sparks awareness as if the only thing keeping him in this world is the thought of knowing I'm safe. I'll give him that peace. It may be the last time I'll be able to offer him any kind of peace before he's ripped from my arms.

"I will take care of myself." Before I kiss him again, I add, "I promise." Internally, I scream, making myself a different promise altogether, hoping that nature—begging nature to side with me.

If he's a star and the night is claiming him, I want the night to take us both.

I undo the buttons of his shirt, desperate to feel his skin against mine, to take some of the tremors shaking his body upon me. I kiss him again.

"Aimee, stop. I shouldn't kiss you... I don't want you to get sick... please."

"I won't. Kiss me, Tristan. It's the only way I will be all right."

I lose myself in the warmth of his lips and the weakness of his body as he kisses me sweetly, though it feels more like goodbye to the thousands of kisses that will never be ours. I kiss him again and again, hoping to catch his disease. Hoping that whatever will keep him from opening his eyes and drawing a breath tomorrow morning, will take me as well. Maybe his disease is not from the mosquitoes, but from something he can indeed pass on to me.

I hope so.

Later, I rest with my head on his chest, neither of us speaking. The sound of pain fills the silence. It's less intense than before, and I think I know why. Fear numbs it now. I remember the power of fear of the unknown. I remember waiting, crouched on my bed, for news of my parents after I learned the revolution had begun. I *needed* to find out if they were all right. It terrified me, imagining scenario after scenario. I wanted to know what happened to them. If they were still alive. I thought nothing would be worse than the uncertainty.

But the pain of losing them was a million times worse.

I wish I could pour some of my life into Tristan. Maybe that could buy him a few hours, a few days. Since there is no way I can do that, I hold out the hope that my own life will trickle out of me at the same time his leaves him. People enter and leave your life all the time; I've learned that long ago. But I've also learned that their loss makes you feel as light and meaningless as the wind yet at the same time your whole existence has an unbearable weight. When they leave, they punch a hole in your existence, and you never feel complete again. The memories they've left you with turn to shadows. You always carry them with you, but they are never whole, and you can never touch them. I've lived surrounded by shadows since my parents died. I can't live in a world where Tristan becomes a shadow too. Without the man who taught me what it feels like to be whole, I become a shadow myself. How lucky to be the one who leaves, and not the one who's left behind.

Everything crumbles inside me when sleep finally overcomes him and he closes his eyes. With every breath and every heartbeat he slips farther away from me. All I can hope for is one more breath, one more heartbeat. So I stay perched above him, listening, drinking each heartbeat in.

My last thought before sleep claims me is that I won't get to hear his last heartbeat.

Chapter 27

Aimee

I dream of a clearing inundated with light with Tristan, healthy and smiling, calling my name. "Aimee." Again and again. I don't open my eyes, too afraid of the reality where nothing more than darkness and silence await me. And no Tristan because, while last night the heat of his feverish body was burning me, there is no longer warmth around me, though I fell asleep in his arms.

That's when I realize he's no longer next to me, but he's indeed calling my name. "Aimee."

I sit up, opening my eyes. Through the dim light I see Tristan hovering near the water basket. I leap toward him. Unable to utter a coherent sentence, I wrap my arms around him, gluing my ear to his chest, hungry to hear his heartbeats. Every muscle in my body mollifies when his rhythmic beats reach me, each one more precious than the last. I burst into tears as the realization of how close I was to never hearing it beat again seeps in.

"It's all right, Aimee. I'm fine. I feel better."

I just cling to him, sobbing.

"Your fever is gone," I say, pulling myself together.

"Apparently so."

"Do you still feel sick?"

"No, just hungry."

"The fever... will it come back?"

"Hard to tell." He shrugs. "No idea what disease I had—my guess is it was caused by a virus transmitted by mosquitoes. I might have a relapse, or I might be immune now to whatever I had. Do you feel all right?"

I nod, beaming. "I just want to stay in your arms for a long time."

So that's what I do.

The disease might have granted us mercy, but the forest didn't. When we disentangle from each other's arms and leave the plane, we see the whole place has been trashed. The fence has numerous holes in it. The rudimentary shelters Tristan and I built for practice are in ruins, bearing traces of fangs and claws at work. This wasn't the doing of just one jaguar.

The mother and her remaining cubs are upon us.

The fact that we killed one of the cubs doesn't seem like a victory anymore now that the rest of the pack is attacking us.

"We prepare for two days," Tristan says. "Then we leave." I don't argue, even though he is weak and I'd like for him to be in excellent shape when we leave. We can't afford to wait any longer. "In the meantime, make sure you carry your bow with you at all times. And stay in my sight." There's no jaguar inside the fence, but I don't feel safe. I shudder... they could be on the other side of the fence. How we'll manage to leave with the pack surrounding us, preparing to attack, I don't know. Tristan wants to mix some of the stored animal fat with blood and smear it on a freshly caught animal. He plans to use that as bait and throw it as far outside the fence as possible, hoping the smell will lure the jaguars long enough to give us time to escape. I'm not convinced it'll work.

I'm not very productive in preparation, because I keep glancing at Tristan every few minutes, terrified he might get sick again. A few months into a new relationship, my friends would often wonder if what they felt toward the guy they were dating was love. How can you tell, they asked me (as if I was somehow a relationship specialist), if he's indeed *the one*. I was in the dark about the answer then, but now I am in the know. You feel complete, and you wonder how you could ever think you were complete before. It's a sensation that fills every pore, every cell with a devastating, almost explosive energy. Like loops of mist after a rain in the forest— it's everywhere.

But another feeling also loiters around. Fear. Terror. Of losing him and that feeling of completeness. Here in the rainforest, where dangers await at every step, this fear follows me. Even more so now, after his illness.

Love has an effect few other things have: to empower you with happiness, and at the same time, strip you of all power, making you a prisoner of fear.

It's late afternoon when Tristan bellows, "Aimee." I spin around, a pit already forming in my stomach. But Tristan isn't alarmed or threatened in any way I can tell. He's staring at something high above us in the distance. I follow his gaze, baffled. The canopy, thick as always, doesn't seem to hold any more threats than usual. I squint my eyes in concentration. And then in the distance, where the canopy is sparser, I see the very thing Tristan sees.

It's not a threat.

It's hope.

In the form of thick, black smoke, rising in swirls up in the sky. Euphoria, the way I don't remember feeling for months, years, perhaps ever, rises from somewhere deep inside me, thick and furious, like the swirls of black smoke I can't take my eyes off.

"What does it mean? Is there a rescue team out there?" I ask.

"We'll find out in a second." Tristan strides toward the plane.

"Where are you going?"

"To get some of those mirror shards I took from the bathroom right after the crash. I can use them to reflect sunlight and send them signals. Keep watch while I get them."

I smile. We're finally a team. I eye the holes in the fence, my fingers tight around the bow, an arrow in place, ready to shoot at a millisecond notice. The swirls of hope inside me turn to tiny, sprinkly bubbles, as if I'm drinking glass after glass of champagne. By the time Tristan returns holding two palm-sized mirror shards, I am drunk on hope. At last, something to look forward to other than a jaguar attack or endless weeks of walking through the rainforest aimlessly. Something good for once. A thread of hope at last.

"I'll climb that tree," Tristan says, pointing to the tree I climbed on our first day. He's also holding a sheet of paper and a pen. They were in the cockpit and we never used those in our poetry sessions because Tristan wanted to save them precisely in case something like this happened, and he needed to write a message. "On second thought, let's both climb it. I don't want you to stay here alone."

Tristan takes the lead, but between trying to be careful with the mirror shards and his weakness, he's slow. On a normal day, he can climb a tree twice as fast as me. Three branches separate us from the top of the tree when Tristan says, "There aren't enough strong branches at the top to sustain both of us. Wait for me here, all right?"

I'd like nothing better than to climb with him, and see the signals he's going to send with my own eyes, but I do as he says. I rest against a branch, careful to stay out of the way of any animal. I lean my head back, looking up at Tristan until I get dizzy and almost fall from the tree.

"What kind of signals are you sending them?" I ask.

"Morse code."

"Will they understand it?"

"If they set out to rescue us they should."

"Have you finished sending the signal?"

"Yes."

"Are they answering?"

Silence.

Sweat claims my skin as minutes pass with no answer. The euphoria from earlier turns to dread.

What if it's not a rescue team after all? What if it's a native tribe that lit up a fire? Tribes can be friendly or hostile. That was always one of the risks awaiting us out here. No, it can't be a tribe. If there was a tribe nearby, we would've realized it before. Unless they migrate. Are there even tribes that do that? Has our own signal fire alerted them of a foreign presence, and they decided to deal with us now?

I take a deep breath, forcing myself to remain calm. An impossible task. Horrifying images of natives and jaguars attacking us play in my mind until I'm so stiff with fear, I doubt I'll be able to move from here if Tristan tells me there is no rescue team after all.

"They're answering," Tristan's voice reverberates through the branches, liquefying me. "They're answering right now." In his voice I recognize the same euphoria that threatens to burst from my chest. I stay silent, much as I'm dying to learn what they're saying. I don't want Tristan to miss one single bit of whatever they are communicating to us. Morse code isn't terribly difficult. Tristan explained it to me the first days after the crash. Each numeral and letter has an equivalent in Morse code—a combination of dots and dashes. One can use a mirror to reflect sunlight to send Morse code signals: moving the mirror quickly to reflect light in dots, and longer movements to reflect light in dashes. It's tricky getting the right angle of reflection, but I have full confidence in Tristan. He taught me how to send an SOS signal. The letter S is made of three dots, and the letter O of three dashes. SOS, or the signal for distress, would mean three dots, three dashes, and three dots. Sending a longer message is possible; it just takes more time. And because it takes so long, it's easy to forget parts of the message if you don't write it down. I'm glad we kept the paper and pen, and that he brought them with him.

We stay up the tree for what feels like hours. It's not until after Tristan says, "Let's go down," that I speak.

"What did they say?"

"I'll tell you everything once we're down. Come on. There are ants up here, and they've already bitten the hell out of me."

I hurry down the tree, and when I'm on the last branch I take a good look around for any sign that the jaguars have returned. Nothing. I leap down, with Tristan on my heels. He leads me to the airstairs, and sitting there, he says, "There is indeed a rescue team out there."

"How far are they from us?" I ask.

He looks down at the piece of paper where he wrote the message.

"They estimate they'll need about two weeks to reach us. If we leave tomorrow morning and keep a fast pace, and they also move toward us, we'll meet in the middle in a week. They have medicine and guns, and they will lead us to a place where a helicopter can pick us up."

"How far is that place?"

"They haven't told me."

"Why can't the helicopter come here to pick us up if they know where we are?"

"They said there is flight prohibition in this area. It must have been instigated after we crashed, because it wasn't prohibited before."

I stare at him. "Why would there be a flight prohibition here?"

"They didn't explain. It's possible they don't know. Prohibition areas are decided by state organizations and they don't always offer explanations for what they do. The fact is, there is no way a helicopter can fly here, not even to drop supplies or pick us up. It will wait for us just outside the perimeter of the prohibited area."

"No one can make an exception for a rescue mission?" I ask incredulously.

"I really don't think anyone views us as a matter of national concern in order to make such an exception. At any rate, maybe the rescue team tried to obtain a permit for bringing a helicopter here and was denied. Or they didn't get an answer yet and grew tired of waiting. Knowing how slow these things are, it could take much longer to obtain a permit than coming here on foot and going back on foot too."

I sigh.

"But it doesn't matter. We are going home, Aimee."

I beam as Tristan carefully folds the piece of paper with the message and tucks it in his pocket.

That's so much more than we could ever hope for. No more walking blindly, hoping against hope it's the right direction. I think of the future, when all that will remain from our time in the rainforest will be our memories. And well, the black scratch on my shoulder. I've been rubbing it every time I shower, but it won't go away. It hasn't lost any of its intensity either. No matter. My bones feel feather-light. The air seems less heavy and moist. I'm grinning like an idiot, but Tristan isn't.

The euphoria that colored his voice earlier still illuminates his face, but with a thin veil of uneasiness underneath it. It might not be recognizable to anyone else, but it is to me. I know Tristan so well, I can read even the smallest of signs. Like a twitch of his eye. The way he rubs the back of his neck with his hand, tugging with his teeth on his lower lip. I search for what might have triggered this but can't figure it out. There's nothing about a rescue team that can cause him anything but joy. Then I realize... there is one thing...

"Who assembled the rescue team, Tristan?" I ask, my palms sweaty all of a sudden.

"Chris. He's with them," Tristan answers, avoiding my gaze. His voice shook when he spoke Chris's name, but his tone turns very brisk when he continues. "You should look through your suitcase, if there is anything that could be of help on the trip. We leave tomorrow morning. I'll hunt for dinner."

"Don't go outside the fence."

"No need to. Plenty of birds within reach here tonight."

Tristan gets up from the airstairs, but I remain propped there for a long time. This is not how I envisioned seeing Chris again. It wasn't supposed to be here in the forest, among the trees and the birds that were silent witnesses to Tristan's and my love. This place belongs to us and us alone. I play a hypothetic conversation with Chris in my head. It doesn't relieve my anxiety. Especially when I remember the ring in my suitcase. No matter what I say, it will be awful. Chris set up an entire team to face the rainforest and rescue his fiancée. And when he finds her, she's in love with someone else. Poor repayment. I can't make things right. Still, I am very thorough in preparing my speech. My defense. My betrayal.

If I had known I wouldn't get the chance to utter one single word of that speech, I would have spent these hours differently.

Chapter 28

Aimee

Early the next day I saunter out of the plane to search for eggs. It'll be our last meal before we leave, and I want it to be nourishing. We have some leftovers from the bird Tristan caught yesterday, but it won't be enough. My stomach constricts at the sight of numerous, fresh paw prints on the ground. Tristan prepares the bait we'll use to lure the jaguars away. I pray it'll work and climb in one of the trees on the inside of the fence, a basket hanging from my left hand. I find enough nests on the upper branches to fill my basket with eggs. My thoughts keep flipping between being so close to safety and my rapidly approaching encounter with Chris. I'm not paying as much attention as I should to my surroundings when I jump down from the tree, my basket filled with eggs. I scan the area for any signs of a jaguar waiting to sink its fangs into me and rip me apart, and seeing none, proceed back to the plane. Or at least I attempt to.

It's not a jaguar that stops me, but a sharp bite on my left ankle. I cry out, dropping the basket. My heart leaps to my throat at about the same time my eyes drop to the ground. My stomach recoils when I find half a dozen black, thin snakes slinking around my feet, two with heads roaring open, ready to sink their teeth into my leg again. I've stepped right into the viper lair I discovered in our first weeks here but forgot about. Adrenaline courses through me as my legs dart forward, not before I feel a second sharp sting. Dizzy with horror and pain, I race to the plane, soon out of breath but afraid to stop, because if I do, the adrenaline sustaining me might succumb to the poison.

"Tristan," I say when I reach the airstairs, leaning against the railing. Heavy beads of sweat trickle down my forehead. Tristan looks at my basketless arms with raised eyebrows, but his bafflement turns into a mask of horror when I point down to my feet. I look down and dart forward, throwing up. The flesh is torn apart where the second viper bit me—no doubt its fangs were still in my flesh when I ran—blood trickling out as the venom trickles in. The sight makes me nauseous, but I don't throw up again. Instead, I lose balance. Tristan catches me just before I hit the ground. He lifts me in his arms, hurrying inside the plane. I try to ignore the pulsing pain in my foot but fail, resorting to biting my fist to keep from screaming.

When Tristan puts me down on my chair, I want to lift my foot up, to get a better look at the wound.

"No," he says, gripping my thigh to keep my leg immobilized. "It's important to keep the injured part below the heart level."

"What now?" I ask.

Tristan runs his hand through his hair, not meeting my eyes. Panic swells in my chest at his silence. "Tristan?" I press. "How do we get the venom out?" I remember reading in a travelling guide never to suck out the poison from a venomous snakebite... or use a tourniquet to stop the venom from spreading. That could cause gangrene. In fact, the guide emphasized not to attempt anything and get to a medical unit as fast as possible, because venom gets into the bloodstream quickly. It seemed like sound advice when I read it. Now it seems a cruel joke. Still, I hold the hope that Tristan has learned some kind of emergency trick during his time in the Army. The desperation in his eyes tells the exact opposite.

"We can't," he says, and despite the fact that his voice appears calm, steady, I can hear cracks starting to tear at his confidence. "But maybe there is no poison."

"No poison?" I raise my voice, partly because a new wave of pain just seared through me, and partly because what he's saying is ridiculous. "Are you forgetting where we are? Even the damn frogs are poisonous here."

"Listen to me. When a poisonous snake strikes, it doesn't always release venom." His voice trembled when he spoke the first words but as he continues, it becomes smoother, almost official. He must have said this before, maybe to one of his comrades when they were on a mission. "But in case venom did enter your bloodstream, it's important that you remain calm so your heart rate doesn't speed up.

That keeps the blood from circulating faster, thus spreading the venom faster."

"And I'm supposed to remain calm knowing this?"

"It's a protection measure, Aimee." His hand caresses my cheeks, and then he pulls me into an embrace. I press my cheek against his chest, losing myself in his arms. For a moment, I believe everything will be all right. Then the pain strikes again. I bite my lip hard to keep from screaming. Tristan's heartbeats are frantic—I don't want him to worry even more. "You most likely have no venom in your blood at all."

"You're not saying that just so I don't panic, are you?"

"No, it's true. That happened a couple of times when we were on missions." I want to believe him. I want to know what happened to those guys, but I'm afraid to ask. Even if they didn't die from the snake bite, chances are bad things happened to them anyway. And I don't want Tristan to think of those days again. I just pulled him out of his nightmares. My desperation to know is not worth losing his peace of mind. "I'm not worried about venom."

I lick my lips, and nod. He brings the alcohol bottle and starts cleaning the wound. He frowns, his eyes probing the bite on my leg, and my heart rate speeds up. He might not be worried about the venom, but he's worried about *something*.

"Can we still leave?" I ask, though I already know the answer.

"That's out of question," he says. "You can't walk." Then he adds, "I could carry you."

"We'd be too slow. And easy prey." We both

fall silent, probably thinking the same thing. We're easy prey here already. "I'll send the rescue team a message: We'll delay leaving for a few days until you recover."

I don't recover. My leg starts swelling in the first few hours, and I hardly sleep for fear I won't wake up or my leg will double in size in my sleep. Tristan doesn't sleep the entire night, just holding me in his arms, checking on my foot every now and again. It turns out the snakes didn't release venom when they bit me—perhaps they weren't venomous at all. If they were, I'd be dead already. But something equally dangerous looms over me nonetheless.

Infection.

Infection was Tristan's worry from the beginning. Since we have no antibiotic, there's no way to stop it from spreading. Disinfecting it with alcohol doesn't do much. The swelling is almost gone by the second morning, but the edges of the wound turn a stomach-churning shade of violet and yellow. Tristan put a bandage on it, and I wear a long dress so I don't see it, but hiding it doesn't make its effects any less noticeable. I can't walk, even with the cane Tristan makes for me. I give up going out of the plane at all. Leaving to meet the rescue group is out of the question. Our best chance is to wait for them here. Except, that's not a good chance—not even a real one. The jaguars will finish us before our rescuers arrive.

They come inside our fence during the day now, too. There are four of them. We are forced to stay in the plane and keep the airstairs raised above the ground. Tristan hunts from the edge of the door.

He develops a clever system to retrieve his prey by binding a thin thread to the end of the arrow. After the speared animal drops to the ground, he pulls in the thread until the prey is in his hands. It doesn't work all the time because the movement catches the jaguars' attention, and sometimes they capture the animal before Tristan manages to pull it up to us. We remain hungry more often than not. We're also permanently thirsty because his system doesn't work to bring the water baskets closer to us, so we collect rain water by lining our old soda cans on the edge of the door and the elevated airstairs. Tristan tried shooting the jaguars, but they are smart. It's as if they can tell the exact moment he releases the arrow, even if they appear to concentrate on something else—like eating our dinner—and get out of the way.

If we can make it until the rescue team arrives, they have guns and can take out the jaguars immediately. But two weeks is a long time to subsist on air and a very long time to resist with an infection this serious. Still, I cling to the hope that I will resist. But the hope withers, day by day.

On the fifth day after the bite, I realize just how unrealistic that hope is. Tristan is in the cockpit and I am alone in the cabin. I drag myself down the aisle toward my suitcase. I need to change my dress because I can't stand the sight of the blood and pus on it. I do my best to hurry so I can get back to my seat before Tristan leaves the cockpit. He insists I don't move at all and would be beside himself if he saw me. But I *need* to move, otherwise I'll grow roots on my seat. Moving hurts like hell, though. I change my dress. The bandage on my foot catches my attention. I haven't looked at the wound in two days. Tristan won't let me, even when he changes the bandages. Biting my lips, I undo it and my heart stops as my eyes try to take in the horror. The image blurs, as tears fill my eyes and realization seeps in.

I will not get better.

I will not last until the rescue team arrives.

I cry out in rage at the unfairness of it all. Tears stream down my cheeks as my whole body starts shaking. I try to calm myself but fail. Why does it matter anymore?

When I hear noise from the cockpit, I remember why calming myself matters. I can't let Tristan see me like this. He must know how bad my wound is. That's why he didn't let me see it. But he must not know how devastated I am. I crawl back to my seat just as Tristan comes out of the cockpit. He doesn't walk my way, but remains at the door of the plane, crouching down with his back to me. I'm grateful I'm sitting in the second row with a row of seats between me and Tristan. It hides me from his view.

"I'll try to get us some food," Tristan calls over his shoulder. "Maybe I'll get lucky."

"Okay," I say. His hunting will give me enough time to pull myself together. I wipe away my tears, but fresh ones burst. Why now? Why couldn't I have died when the plane crashed? Quickly, perhaps even painlessly. Before I became whole in a way I had never been before, only to lose everything. I shake my head, then hide it between my knees. I can't think like this. I will break down and won't be able to piece myself back together. Drawing in deep breaths, I attempt to calm myself. The effort of not crying slices at my chest with excruciating whiplashes, again and again, until I'm convinced the effort itself will be enough to break me down. I bite my arm when sobs overtake me, and give in to the pain and the fear. I let the pain bleed out in silent tears, until I have none left.

"No chance," Tristan says after what feels like hours. "I've shot down a bird, but the jaguars jumped on it right away. As usual, they've cut the thread with their fangs, so I've lost that arrow, too." Watching me with worry he says, "You're hungry, aren't you?"

"To be honest I can't feel the hunger anymore." Side effects of the pain.

"You still have to eat. I'll try going outside to dig for some roots."

"No. Absolutely not. It's too dangerous."

"So is dying from starvation, Aimee."

I almost laugh out loud. My infected wound will see to it that I don't die of starvation.

And then it strikes me. He will.

Stuck here with me, nothing awaits him but death. *We* might be unable to leave. But Tristan isn't. I've seen him move through the forest. He's agile, strong and fast. If he manages to get past the jaguars, he stands a good chance of reaching the rescue group. Without me as a burden, he can reach safety. The thought fuels my hope. I cling to it for dear life. Oh, I cling to it so desperately. Now I have to convince him to leave.

"I have an idea," I say as Tristan lies on his seat with his eyes closed, tired, hungry, and thirsty. "Why don't you go and meet the rescue team?"

"What?" his sharp voice is accompanied by a loud crack as he bolts into a sitting position, his eyes piercing me.

"It's a good idea. You'd have food and be rejuvenated so you could lead them back to the plane and help me." I don't meet his eyes when I utter the last part, but Tristan can probably read my true intentions. "I know how you move through the forest, Tristan. You can do this better on your own. Even if I were healthy, I'd hold you back. I'm slow and clumsy."

"We're a team, Aimee. You said that."

I sigh. "Well, this would be for the benefit of the team. If you can lead them here quicker, I can receive medical aid quicker."

"I am not leaving you here," he says. "I'm not leaving you at all."

"But you are starving, Tristan. You can't wait for them to reach us." To reach him; by the time the rescue team arrives, I will be dead. He knows that. I know that. Neither of us says it out loud.

He kneels in front of me taking both my hands in his, and then puts them on the sides of his neck. "Remember what you told me when I was sick?"

"I remember we had a thorough astronomy class," I say. At his quizzical look I add, "We talked a lot about stars."

"You said that if I didn't wake up tomorrow, you didn't want to wake up either." His voice is breathy and shaky, as if he's trying to withhold tears "Now I'm telling you that. If you don't make it until the rescue team arrives, I don't want them to rescue me at all." He slings his arms around me in a tender embrace. "But you'll be all right, Aimee. You'll see."

I do see. I see the truth. He's in danger because of me. I'm a liability. I will get worse. That's what infections do. I can't help him fight the jaguars, and we can't leave. We can't do anything because of me. And he won't leave. Disease will rot me, and hunger and thirst will rot him, because he won't leave.

In this flash of a second, with my ear pressed against his chest, I understand what must happen for Tristan to leave.

I have to die.

Chapter 29

Aimee

Since the flesh on my ankle seems to disintegrate with each passing hour, and the pain intensifies at the same rhythm, one would assume I wouldn't have long to live. But death doesn't come as fast as I need it to. After two days of waiting to die, I search for ways to deliberately put myself in danger. It's not easy under Tristan's watchful eyes. I could take a knife and finish myself. I am in so much pain I would welcome any kind of relief. But Tristan has enough survivor guilt to torment himself, I don't need to add more. If I did that, I would take away from him the little freedom he gained in our time together. I try to stop drinking water, but Tristan makes sure I drink to the last drop, insisting I have to hydrate myself. My fever is dangerously high. The air in the plane is becoming sticky and heavy, impossible to breathe.

We haven't eaten anything in a day and a half, and

the prospect of having a meal soon is nonexistent. Tristan's been trying to catch a bird. He's doing fine with the shooting part. The problem is when he pulls the thread at the end of the arrow. That doesn't work because, as usual, the jaguars capture the prey on the way. But Tristan doesn't give up. He shot one bird already today and is on his way to shooting the second. He tries not to shoot more than once a day because we don't have enough arrows. If he uses one arrow a day, we could theoretically last until the rescue team arrives. Unless he doesn't get us a meal with one arrow... then we might starve before the rescue team arrives. He hasn't succeeded yesterday, or today. I suppose that prompted him to use a second arrow today.

I stay curled in my seat, fighting sleep and exhaustion. It creeps in every single bone. Every time I wipe sweat from my forehead I'm reminded of the reason for my unnatural exhaustion. My fever is so high my brain must be fried. I eventually give in and drowse.

"Finally," Tristan announces, startling me. "Oh, look, the poor bird fell in your spine bush by the entrance when I shot it."

"Huh?" I ask, still fighting the tendrils of sleep.

"The spines with the black sap."

Through watery eyes I see Tristan pluck out a handful of spines from the bird's plumes. They are indeed the same kind of spines that left the black line on my shoulder. Tristan's gaze darts from the bird to me.

"How are you feeling Aimee?" The worry in his tone acts as an impulse. I force myself to sit straighter.

"Just a bit tired," I lie.

"Does your leg hurt?"

"It's not that bad today." This is not a lie. Either I'm so beyond pain I don't recognize it anymore (which I admit, is a realistic possibility) or the fever has somehow numbed me.

Tristan starts a very small fire just at the edge of the cracked door, roasting the bird. When we realized we would be forced to retreat inside the plane, we brought as much wood as possible inside.

After the bird is roasted, we eat it up hungrily. Then Tristan picks up one of the three cans lining the elevated airstairs. They contain the precious portion of water we can collect every day. As usual, Tristan drinks just a few gulps, then attempts to make me drink the rest.

"You should drink more water." I push away his hand holding the can to my lips.

"You need to hydrate. Your fever—"

"My fever will kill me anyway," I say. Tristan's hand freezes in mid-air, his knuckles turning white. "Let's not pretend, Tristan, just this one time."

"I can't... I don't want to think like this, Aimee. There is still a chance they will reach us in time."

"Tristan." His name spills out my lips with urgency. I want to say it as often as I can in the time I have left. "We both know even if that happens, the hike to the helicopter will take too long. I'll never survive."

He flinches hard. I shouldn't have been so blunt. I'm the one who's accepted my death after all. He hasn't.

"I'm sure they have medicine with them," Tristan says. That has to be true. But my blood poisoning needs more than what a mobile arsenal can carry. No, what I need can only be found in a hospital. But his tone is so hopeful there's no doubt he's not faking it. This is not good. The sooner he lets go of hope and accepts truth, the better—the faster he'll recover when the inevitable happens. I open my mouth, then close it again, not sure how to put this in words. I can't find it in myself to break him. I don't know what's crueller: letting him hope, or robbing the hope from him.

As if guessing what's on my mind, he presses his lips to mine, and no more words slip out. He sits next to me, and I melt in his kiss, losing myself in his taste and warmth, allowing my skin to tingle with need for him, and my body to soak up his proximity. My hands roam his body, driven by a will of their own—they caress his hard abdomen, the sharp ridges of his hipbones, and travel all the way to his back. He has become so thin. His hands travel over me with equal intensity. There's no restraint in his touch anymore. Since I was bitten, he's restrained, as if he's afraid his kisses or touch might break me. But not now. I revel in the feeling. His passion burns away every thought and worry. Like a balm, it runs through the cracks that have splintered me these last few days in which I tried to keep my pain hidden from him.

"You're everything to me, you know that? You always will be," he whispers against my lips. Tendrils of reality raze at me at the word *always*, but I push them away. I don't want to bring reality up this very second. I refuse to lose what is mine for certain— the present—by worrying over a future I have no control over.

"Always?" I ask in a playful tone. "That's a serious statement right there."

He gazes at me with warm eyes. "Always. I would marry you in a heartbeat and take care of you until we're both old, wrinkly, and nagging. I'd brew you coffee every morning and hold you tightly in my arms every night. It would be a privilege to watch you fall asleep every night. I can't imagine anything more beautiful and fulfilling than growing old next to you and taking care of you. Always loving you."

My heart skips a beat at the impossible beauty of his words. "Tristan, I..." Words fail me, as usual.

"Would you say yes?" His eyes search mine with chilling urgency, and he inches closer to me. I feel the caress of his warm breath on my lips. "Would you marry me if we were in another place, and I could give you a big wedding, like the one you always dreamed of?"

I push him away, playfully. "No way."

His breath hitches, pain shadowing his gaze. I didn't come off as playful. "I wouldn't want a big wedding," I continue, "I'd want a small, intimate one."

"Yeah?" The corners of his lips tug upwards in a smile. "After which you'd run away to solve a big case."

I frown. "I wouldn't want to solve cases anymore, or be a lawyer."

"Really?"

"No, I... I'd want to do something else."

"There's a good chance I'd reconsider piloting for a living."

"You, sir, would never get on a plane again. Ever." I kiss him, pulling him closer to me. "You could give that doctor thing a try."

"Nah, I'm too old," he whispers when we break off.

"You are twenty-eight. That is in no way old."

"So you would marry me?"

"I would."

"You said wouldn't want a big wedding... how would you like our wedding to be? Where would you want it to be?"

I lay my head on his chest, trying to envision what that day would look like. "Hmm, somewhere outside, with just a few close friends attending. To be honest, I'd love it if it was just the two of us, but I know a few people who wouldn't forgive me for not inviting them. I'd like to wear a simple dress and be surrounded by lots of flowers, exotic ones like the ones here, if we could get them." After a pause I add, "And I'd like to get one of those tattoos you said natives do."

Tristan tilts my chin up until I look at him. He's grinning. "I thought you found it barbaric."

"Because at the time I didn't understand what it meant to want to give yourself to someone completely. I do now." He pulls me up to him. I wish he wouldn't, because a tear has found its way down my cheek, and I want to hide it. Tristan catches it with his thumb, glancing at it stricken.

"Aimee," he whispers, and in this moment, all I can think of is what a privilege it is to hear him say my name, and how very few times I have to enjoy the luxury of hearing him say it. I hate it. Most of all, I hate there will never be a wedding. I'll never stay next to him in white, exchanging vows. The longing to do that hits me fast, and so hard it wipes the air from my lungs. If I could have one last wish granted, it would be to do that. I don't understand why it's suddenly so important, but it would give me the peace I lost when I realized I won't make it out of here. When Tristan looks at me, he reads my thoughts. I see he wants to reassure me that it's not true, that I'll have lots of time—months, years—to hear him say my name. But now I'm the one who doesn't let him say anything. To silence him, I press my mouth to his, allowing his lips to envelop me with that wonderful power they have to wipe away every thought. I'm glad we had this conversation. I know how important it was to him. When you are healthy you think you have all eternity to say what matters. When you're sick you learn how to live every moment, and how to make every moment matter. How sad that we learn this when we're about to run out of time. I would have never told him this if I were healthy. Embarrassment and inhibition have always kept me from expressing my deepest desires, hopes, and thoughts. I guess in a way, I cannot consider my illness a complete curse.

We break apart, gasping for air, and then he wraps me in a tight embrace, kissing my forehead. "Well, if you want to be surrounded by lots of exotic flowers, we'd better pack a handful of them when we leave this place," he says jokingly. Then he leaps to his feet. I pull myself up straighter, my heart hammering a million miles an hour as I look around, trying to find what alerted him. I don't see anything that could pose a threat.

"We could do it here," he says.

"Do what here?" I ask blankly.

"Get married." He cups my face in his hands.

"There are more than enough flowers, and you have a white dress. The one you didn't want to wear because it was too long. Kind of hard to get rings, but we could do without them for now. We have some of those spines with coloring sap," he says, pointing to the stack of spines he plucked from the bird. "We can use them for the tattoos. What do you say?" I fumble with the buttons of his shirt, fighting tears. He can't possibly understand how much this means to me.

"Cold feet already so soon after saying yes? What do you say, Aimee?" he beckons me to answer.

"I'd love that," I whisper.

He presses his lips on my forehead. "I'll sneak out to bring some flowers..."

"No way. I've memorized all the flowers on the inside of the fence anyway. I'll just imagine we have them here."

"I'll help you change in your white dress after I change. Or do you want to me to help you before?"

"No, no... I'll change on my own."

"But you can't—"

"Please, Tristan. I'd like to do this myself."

"All right."

He goes inside the cockpit, a feeling fluttering in my stomach. Since I can barely move, I crawl to my suitcase, gritting my teeth as pain sears my leg with even the lightest movement. I refuse to look at my leg and put on the white dress with dark blue lace, thankful for its length. I'll have to make sure it doesn't slide sideways, revealing my leg. That would be a definite mood-killer. I comb my hair, letting it fall on my back. It feels strange after the months I've worn it in a bun. I find the makeup bag

I stuffed at the bottom of the suitcase when we first made an inventory of what we had. I forgot I had it. I open it, and in the small mirror on the inside of the cap, I see my reflection and gasp. I look horrible, like someone sucked the life out of me. My skin is a sickly pale color. I must have lost far more weight than I thought, because my cheekbones are very prominent. They make the deep, dark circles under my eyes look even more haunting. I sigh, biting my lip. I wish Tristan could remember me beautiful. It's a silly wish to have right now, but I don't care. He has enough ugly memories.

I eye the makeup bag. Maybe I can work with this, though I doubt any amount of makeup can make me look beautiful now. My spirits lift a tad as I start applying makeup. The fluttering feeling becomes more intense, filling me more and more as I apply concealer under my eyes, and put a light blush on my cheeks. By the time I smear lipstick on my lifeless lips, I'm certain I will burst with excitement. The image in the mirror gradually becomes alive. By the time I'm done, I'm far from beautiful, but I no longer look like a corpse. It takes me forever to crawl back to my seat. After pondering for a few seconds whether this is the best place to sit, I crawl to the space in front of the door. We'll have more room here. I'm attempting to clean the spot by pushing aside the remnants of thread Tristan uses to tie the end of the arrows, when an idea strikes me. I put some of the thread between my fingers and weave it in a surprise for Tristan. When he comes out of the cockpit, I hide my secret behind my back. My breath catches. He's wearing his uniform with a freshly washed, white shirt underneath.

"Wow. You look beautiful, Aimee."

My face warms as his gaze rakes over me, drinking me in. "Thank you." I check whether the dress covers my hurt leg. "So do you."

"I had a tie somewhere, but can't find it. Why are you holding your hands behind your back?"

"None of your business," I say cheekily.

"What are you hiding?" He grins, and takes a step toward me, trying to peek behind my back. I jerk, pressing my elbow on my hurt leg. I wince from the pain, and Tristan's grin drops. I force a smile on my face, even though the pain is so sharp that my eyes begin to water. "Shhh, don't look. It's a surprise. Go find your tie."

He looks at my covered leg, but I shake my head, smiling. "Go find it, before I change my mind about marrying you." The second he's out of sight I let my pain out through gritted teeth. There is a blood stain on my dress from where I pressed on my leg. I don't dare look under my dress. I rearrange the dress so the stain isn't visible.

Tristan takes forever, and I begin to wonder if something happened to him, or if he changed his mind, when he comes out. His tie in place, I don't think I have ever loved him more than when he sits in front of me, saying, "Ready to be mine forever?"

I smile. "Ready."

He takes my hands. "I haven't prepared any elaborate vows, but I... I would love for you to be my wife. It will be a privilege to love you more every day. I will not take your love for granted, but give you new reasons to fall in love with me every day. I will learn all the ways to make you smile and make sure the only kind of tears you spill are ones of happiness."

A knot forms in my throat, and when Tristan indicates it's my turn to speak, I chuckle.

"You hadn't prepared any vows, huh?" I whisper, searching for words, but only finding tears. He spoke so beautifully of a future we won't have.

"Hey, we can skip your vows and go straight to the kiss."

"No, you can't kiss me yet," I say.

At his puzzled expression, I bring out my hands from behind my back and hold them out to him. In my palm are two gray rings woven out of thread. He puts one between his fingers, and for a moment seems unable to speak.

"You like them?" I ask nervously. "I just wanted us to have something resembling rings—"

"They're perfect."

He's the first to push the ring on my finger, and I hold my breath, my whole body shaking with fulfilling, exhilarating happiness. As I push the larger ring on his finger, I see the thread has started to rot away already. The ring will wither away before long. Just like me. Perhaps it's a good thing. No permanent reminder of me. This way, he can recover quicker after I'm gone. Tristan's lips clash against mine when I secure the ring on his finger. His kiss isn't gentle or restrained like the ones grooms give their brides. He cups my head in his palms, his tongue ravaging mine. He kisses me like he knows he doesn't have many kisses left.

Afterward I ask, "Can you bring the spines?"

"Just a sec." He places the pile of spines on one of the old magazines I must have re-read at least ten times. My vision is so blurry it's hard to distinguish one letter from the other on the magazine cover. That's when I know my fever is impossibly high. My heart pounding in my throat, I focus harder on the letters. A stream of hot tears bursts down my cheeks. I hope he thinks it's from emotion.

"Should I do yours first?" Tristan asks.

"Absolutely."

"How about I put the first letter of my name?"

"No. I want your whole name. It's beautiful."

"Are you sure?"

I nod.

"All right. Here we go."

While Tristan puts the dripping tip of the spine on my upper arm, I study his features. The arch of his brows, the curl of his long lashes, his lips. I want to memorize every detail about him, while I can still see through the blurs. Feeling the spine on my skin doesn't hurt at all. It gives me a giddy feeling of completion that is replaced by horror when Tristan puts another spine in my hand, saying, "Your turn. I want to get your whole name, too."

"No," I say, terrified. "Why not just the first letter or something else? You said natives use symbols sometimes..."

"I want us to match. Go on," he beckons, rolling up the sleeve of his shirt, revealing his upper arm. I mentally curse as I write my name on his skin. I shouldn't have brought tattooing up. A permanent reminder of my name is the last thing he needs. I only want him to remember how I made him feel. Nothing more.

I feel dizzy when I finish, and lie on the floor, with my head in his lap. I close my eyes as he threads his fingers through my hair. Each movement of his fingers, each breath seems to last an eternity. I no longer resent I won't have more time for moments like this. In fact, I no longer feel like I am out of time.

When you are on the brink of the great unknown, when you're so close to the edge of the abyss you can almost bite into the darkness, time acquires something of a magical quality to it. You start measuring time in seconds, and all of a sudden, each second lasts forever.

Death has its beauty.

It makes you see the eternity in every second; it makes you see every moment's perfection instead of searching an eternity for the perfect moment.

Time moves differently—beautifully—for those who only have smidgens of it left. But there is no beauty in death for those left behind. When I open my eyes, I find Tristan looking at me. I try to avoid it, because there is no mistaking the pain in his eyes. I know that pain. I remember how it felt to watch over him, thinking how lucky he was for being the one who got to leave first, and how unlucky I was to be the one left behind. I am the lucky one now. The fever exhausts me, and I soon have to fight to keep my eyes open.

"I love you, Aimee," Tristan whispers. "So much." Cracks shatter his voice, finding their way deep into him. I know how those cracks feel. When he was sick, they splintered me too, in that terrifying way only pain can. Now I'm too weak to move, there is no pretending. Nowhere to run from the truth. Or in my case, the end.

In a blur, I raise my hand, touching his cheek. I find tears on it. Lowering my hand on his chest, I realize he's shaking.

He's losing it.

I'm glad the fever is tampering with my vision, because I can't see him like this. Not when I know there is nothing I can do to alleviate the pain of this man who has given me so much.

"I love you too," I say in a weak whisper. He hugs me to his chest. Despite the fact that I am barely aware of my surroundings, the rhythm of his heartbeats reaches me. Clear and loud. They sound like scattered fragments of hopes and dreams. With a shift that claims my very last drops of energy, I push myself up to meet his lips, hoping I can transfer some of my peace to him.

As I feel the warmth of his lips, I become greedy. Suddenly, an eternity is not enough, and his cracks become mine. The fragments slashing at him slash at me too, until tears stream on my cheeks as well, mingling with his. The fervor of our lips is not enough to build a shield around us. Inside it, we would be protected from the truth.

I give myself completely to him with this kiss, like I have with all the kisses before. Every kiss, caress, and word of his has claimed a part of me; now I belong more to him than to myself. One stolen kiss, one gifted smile, one shared memory at a time.

Chapter 30

Aimee

There is no wedding night because, still lying in Tristan's arms, I succumb to the fever. A heavy sleep overcomes me the moment I close my eyes. After that, days and nights morph into an endless spiral of pain and despair. My body shuts down systematically. Tristan tries to feed me, but my throat forgets how to swallow. My whole body rejects food. Soon, it starts rejecting water too, though it needs it. Oh, so much. I can feel myself cremating from the inside, scorching away until there is a bitter taste of ash in my mouth. And then comes the moment when I feel no hunger or thirst. I know I'm in real trouble when I can't even feel the pain anymore. What grounds me to the world is the intake of air—a whiff of forest air or the smell of Tristan's skin, indicating he's nearby.

I start praying for my body to reject the air, too, along with everything else. Tristan talks to me, but I can't make sense of his words. Of course, that could just be my imagination; maybe Tristan is not talking to me at all, too weak from hunger, or hurt by the jaguars. But if it's a mirage, I'll gladly stick to it.

I know my brain has succumbed to madness when I start hearing voices. Lots of them. Frantic and loud. I try to ignore them at first, because hearing voices in my head is not a dignified way to leave this world. But then I start paying attention. I recognize more than one voice. For the first time, I become aware that at least one part of my body is still functioning: my heart. It slams against my ribcage, reminding me I'm still alive.

For now.

I open my eyes, and force them to stay open for a few seconds, but I get dizzy fast, and my eyes start watering. I push myself up my elbows, but my fever-fried brain perceives this as a disruption equal to an earthquake, and I become nauseous. I can't make sense of much other than there are many people milling around in the plane. People I don't know.

Two of them crouch in front of me, and one of them shouts something over his shoulder. It might have been, *She woke up*.

I look down at my hands, and I see needles in my veins, and an infusion bag next to me. The rescue team must have arrived. I don't have time to rejoice, because I collapse on my back, my eyes sewing themselves together so tightly I can't open them again, hard as I try. I cling to my senses with my last ounce of energy: to the smell of the forest present in the plane, to the sound of voices calling to me, some with desperation, some hopeless. One with quiet urgency. Tristan's. I can't make out his whispered words, but when he interlaces his fingers with mine, I cling to him.

The last words I hear before I slide into a coma are, "She won't make it."

They belong to Chris.

Chapter 31

Tristan

The rescue team tells me how they learned we were still alive. A few weeks ago a new flight destination was added to the Manaus airport, which passed just outside the prohibition area. Aimee and I were in the visual range of that flight's route. A plane flying on the route noticed the black smoke from the fire Aimee insisted on lighting regularly. The airport instructed the planes flying that route to monitor the area, fearing that it might be a forest fire, doubting the smoke came from a signal fire. After a few more planes reported that the fire hadn't extended, they didn't doubt that it was a signal fire anymore. No plane except ours had crashed in the Amazon in the last five years. They knew it must be us.

The rescue team takes out the jaguars easily with a few shots. They can't take care of Aimee as easily. She is half dead. There is a doctor on the team, but he doesn't have the necessary equipment and medicine with him to save her. We set out on foot almost immediately after they arrive, but the place the helicopter is allowed to land is still days away. Chris tells me he tried to obtain a permit to bring the helicopter inside the prohibition area, but failed, despite bribing and calling in favors from everyone. Coming with a car was also impossible, because the trees are too close to each other. Chris and I carry her on a stretcher. He learned about *us* the minute he entered the plane—his eyes fell on her name scribbled on my shoulder, and my name on hers. He acknowledged it with a stunned expression but didn't speak about it. Now it's all about saving her. I hold on to the hope that we'll reach the hospital in time. But as I watch the woman who means the world to me become weaker by the second, that hope turns to ash.

Life scorches away from her with every step.

Chapter 32

Aimee

Light blinds me when I open my eyes. It's so bright I cross both my arms over my eyes. The darkness calms me. I inhale deeply, but the smell travelling down my throat, filling my lungs, alarms me. It's not the heavy and moist smell of the forest. It's light, tinted with the aroma of alcohol. I search for a strand of familiar. Something to indicate that Tristan is nearby. The smell of his skin. The heat of his body. No trace of either. He's not nearby. Where is he, then? The way to find out is to put my arms down and face whatever is in front of me. It can't be worse than what I left behind—the forest. My leg doesn't hurt anymore. In fact, no part of my body aches. If I'm all right, then Tristan must be as well.

I lower my arms slowly, allowing my eyes to get accustomed to the bright white surrounding me. The ceiling. The walls. The bed sheet and my hospital gown. My heart rate intensifies by the second, the more I take in my surroundings, familiar and strange at the same time. I graze the bed sheet with my fingernails. The softness of the fabric and the smell of fresh and clean almost bring tears to my eyes.

One of the few spots of color comes from the screen of the vital signs monitor next to my bed. On the tray under the screen are at least five different types of pills. I don't remember taking any.

I turn my head in the other direction, to the window. The sight outside would have kept my attention for longer than a few seconds, if not for the sight beneath the window. An orange couch is there. And on that couch is someone who can bring me both relief and dread. Chris. I draw in a sharp breath. He's sleeping sitting up, his head bent slightly backward, a few curls of his light blond hair falling over his eyes and cheekbones. I frown as I inspect the dark circles under his eyes; his overall gaunt appearance. Even in sleep—a time when I always thought he looked no more than twenty—he looks years older than when I left him, though just four months have passed. He's wearing a simple blue polo shirt and jeans. I try hard to recall the speech I prepared when I was in the forest, but before I can, he wakes up, his blue eyes focusing on me.

"Hi," he says. For one brief moment I think he will rise and hug me. But he stays put. So do I, though there is nothing restraining me to the bed. Except my conscience.

"Hi."

"You took a long nap."

"How long?"

"Almost a week. You were in the intensive care

unit for a few days, then they brought you here. You kept sleeping. The nurses woke you up several times a day so you could take your pills, but you weren't coherent."

"Where are we?"

"Home. We're in L.A. We took you to the nearest hospital in Brazil, in Manaus. As soon as you were stable I had you flown here. This is the best equipped hospital in L.A. for these kind of cases."

Of course, always the best for me. Shame crashes over me in waves.

"Thank you," I say weakly, and then I say nothing more. All the explanations—excuses—seem too lame now to utter. Too hurtful. I don't want to open my mouth at all, because I'm afraid my most ardent question will slip out: where is Tristan?

Deep down, I'm certain Chris knows everything. Otherwise he'd be next to me, hugging and kissing me. Holding me tight to him.

"Don't you want to know if you'll make a full recovery?"

"Sure," I answer, grateful for a safe topic, but I don't take in his explanation, because the movement of a crane outside the window in the distance captures my attention.

"Can you... can you open the window?" I ask.

Chris stops talking, and I realize I've interrupted him. But he opens the window. The noise outside is like a shock to my system. For a few seconds, I fear my eardrums will pop, but they adjust, and then Chris snaps the window closed.

"You should take it easy. There are lots of people here to see you. Maggie, half a dozen of our friends."

I tear my gaze from the crane outside and focus

it on his shoes. I swallow hard, trying to find the courage to ask him about the person I want to see most.

He spares me the question. "Tristan is here too. Waiting anxiously for you to wake up."

Without meeting his eyes I ask, "How is he?"

"Tristan is in perfect shape. The doctors made sure of that. He's just waiting for the woman he loves to wake up."

It's here at last. The moment of truth. I raise my gaze to meet his. "How do you know?"

Chris smiles. "You have his name inked on your skin, and he has yours. The few times the nurses woke you up you did nothing but call for him. I know because I was right next to you the first few times. Until I couldn't take it anymore and left him at your side. "

"Chris..."

"Don't," he turns his back to me sharply. Hands in his pockets, he stares at the white wall. "I don't blame you and I don't resent you. But I don't want to hear all the reasons you fell in love with him." I remain silent. "You never loved me the way you love him, did you?"

I shake my head, then realize he can't see me. It takes all I have to mutter, "It's different—" He cuts me off.

"Good. That means he must make you very happy. That's what I always wanted for you."

Tears break out, running down my cheeks. I remove the cover from my feet, but find that I can't move without a sharp pain in my left ankle where the snakes bit me. I haven't made a full recovery yet, it seems. I remain in my bed.

"How are you, Chris?"

"Dreadful. I spent the past four months wanting to die because I thought you were dead. Then I find you, but you're not mine to love anymore." His breathy voice undoes me. I bite the inside of my cheek until I taste blood to keep from bursting into more tears. "I lost my fiancée somewhere in the rainforest, didn't I, Aimee?" He chooses the hardest moment of all to spin around and face me. I suppose he wants to look right at me when I deliver the final blow. I can't blame him for that.

"But not your best friend, Chris. She's still here."

He nods, one single tear rolling down his cheek.

"I need time, Aimee. To adjust to all this."

"I understand. I wish I could give you the ring back, but I... I suppose you left my suitcase in the forest. I put the ring in it. I couldn't wear it anymore."

"I wouldn't have expected it any other way."

"I did wear it for a long time. It reminded me of us—"

"Until you didn't want to be reminded of us anymore." It breaks me to be reminded of how well he knows me. "I debated leaving the moment the doctors said you were out of any danger. I thought of leaving you a letter. But I needed closure before I left."

I gulp. "Where are you going?"

"New York. The subsidiary there has needed my attention for some time. Now's a good time to fly there for a prolonged stay."

"You don't have to leave because of this... I... Tristan and I can leave."

"No need. I already made arrangements."

"Chris..." I beg. The thought of losing my best

friend terrifies me. But what can I ask of him? Nothing.

He comes to my bed, sitting on its edge, next to me. I search for words to console him, but none come. There is nothing I can tell the man who has been by my side since childhood and who has never been anything but kind to me. In his clear blue eyes I can see that he doesn't want my words. So I keep them to myself. I'll put them in a letter and send it to him later. In it, I will lay out all my thanks and all my sorrys. "I promise I will return when I am able to think of you as simply my best friend. Until then, my place is not here." He leans in, kissing my forehead. His lips still on my forehead he mutters, "Now, it's high time to tell Tristan you're up."

When Chris walks to the door, the anticipation of seeing Tristan is overshadowed by a deep sense of loss. Chris doesn't say it, but after walking out that door, I know I won't see him again for a long time. I look elsewhere when he exits, and I don't glance at the door again until I hear it crack open and a familiar voice whispers, "Aimee."

The sound drizzles warmth all over my skin, sprinkling beads of happiness, relief, and so much more. Though still thin, he's wearing fresh clothes, his skin boasting a healthy glow I haven't seen on him in months.

There are deep laugh lines around his eyes, because he's smiling ear to ear, his dark eyes glinting. He looks like a different person. Almost. He hasn't cut his hair; the dark waves still brush his shoulders. I take all this in no more than a fraction of a second, because then I lose myself in Tristan's kiss, and his arms as he hugs me. I can't stop my fingers from threading through his hair, nor can I get enough of his warmth and smell. They bring familiarity drop by drop into a world that now feels foreign.

"I love you so much, Aimee," he whispers between kisses, his hands caressing me. "I was so afraid I would lose you."

"I'm all right now. I'm fine," I whisper back. I push a strand of his hair behind his ear, revelling in the feeling of having him this close, unharmed. How wonderful it is not to fear that something might happen to snatch him away from me for good. "There are no more reasons to be afraid." Chuckling, I add, "Except opening windows. I thought I'd have a heart attack when I heard the noise outside."

Tristan smiles. "Don't worry, I felt the same way the first two days. Everything seems alien. But it gets better. I'll be right next to you to make it better."

"You will?"

"Yes. Always. We'll face everything the way we faced the rainforest. Together."

Chapter 33

Aimee

Ten years later

The last rays of sun tap through the window, their reflections creating a rainbow in my champagne glass. Today is a day for celebrating. One way or another, we celebrate every day. But today is special. I arrived home earlier from work to prepare a fancy meal. If I was still a lawyer, that wouldn't have been possible. I never even thought of going back to my old job. Something Tristan told me in the rainforest stuck with me. I can help in my own way. One person at a time. At age twenty-six I ditched what could have been a brilliant career as a lawyer and enrolled at college again—this time to study psychology. A number of friends criticized my decision, but I've learned not to care. It's never too late for a fresh start. Tristan followed suit and enrolled to study medicine. It turns out we both made the right choice, feeling fulfilled with our careers.

The college years, and the ones after, resembled our time in the rainforest in one aspect. It felt like it was just the two of us, making our way in a place we didn't belong. I wish we could be together at all times, like in the forest. Whenever we are apart for more than a day, somewhere deep inside me the irrational fear that something happened to him roars to life. It's normal—I've learned that in my studies. It's a feeling I will never lose, but I can live with it. And when Tristan's arms envelop me, and his lips feather on mine, like they do right now, I forget about it.

"Happy tenth unofficial anniversary," he murmurs against my lips, clinking the champagne glass he's holding against mine. I admire my husband's beauty before answering. His black hair is now peppered with two white streaks I adore. His dark eyes haven't lost any of their glint.

"It's the official one for me." We had an official wedding a month after our return from the rainforest. We had gold wedding rings and everything. But each year, we celebrate our anniversary on the day we exchanged the thread rings in the forest. Today is our tenth. Every year on this day we take out the glass box where we keep those thread rings. The box is our little glass bubble, preserving the purity of the forest and the strength of our love.

The thread rings have been eroded by the years; they're fragile. We never remove them from the box, afraid we might damage them. We just look at them and clink champagne glasses over the box. We save wearing them for an unknown special occasion.

Neither of us knows when that occasion will be, but we are certain we'll recognize it when it arrives. The tattoos we made in the forest faded over the years, but they are still readable. We thought about getting them re-done, this time in an actual tattoo parlor, but decided against it. It just wouldn't feel the same.

"Mom, Mom." The voice resounds from the little garden outside our house. It belongs to a five-year-old girl with Tristan's black hair and my green eyes. I glance at her through the open door of the kitchen. She's running from the entrance gate on the patio, taking both steps leading to our porch in one jump. When she arrives in the kitchen, she's out of breath, clutching a rectangular box wrapped in brown paper against her chest.

"Look what the mailman brought," she says proudly. "From Uncle Chris."

"How do you know it's from him?" Tristan asks, feigning suspicion. He's suppressing a smile.

"It says right here." She places her tiny finger on the envelope where the name of the sender is written. "I can read all the letters of the alphabet."

"You can, huh?" Tristan takes her in his lap, tickling her until she roars with laughter. It's contagious, and all three of us end up laughing with guffaws.

"I think it's another porcelain doll," she says after we calm down, her eyes brimming with hope. "For my collection."

"Well, what are you waiting for? Open it," I beckon. She rips the brown paper, revealing indeed, a porcelain doll.

"When will he visit us again?" she asks.

"Let's call and ask him, shall we?" Tristan says, lifting Lynda in his arms. On a whim, I rise on my toes and give him a kiss. A light one, the way we always exchange kisses when Lynda can see us. Tristan winks at me as he steps out to the porch with Lynda to call Chris.

It took a long time for Chris and I to connect again. I sent an email to him with all my thoughts and apologies the day before I married Tristan. I never got an answer, but I didn't expect one. I didn't attempt to make any contact for a few years afterward. Not until I saw a picture of him in the news—he had received an award for business innovator of the year. On his arm was a beautiful, blonde woman. I thought it might be safe to write to him again. He was still in New York. We emailed back and forth for a few months and after she became his wife they visited us for the first time. I was enchanted with her, and they were both enchanted by Lynda. Gradually, I got my best friend back, Tristan gained a friend, and Lynda had someone to call Uncle. It went smoother than I expected. Smoother than many other things we had to fight for. My health, for example. Despite the doctor's best efforts (and mine during the recovery therapy), I'm left with a slight limp in my leg and a scar where I was bitten.

Some days my leg hurts, and I can do nothing more than curl up with a book. We have a library full of books. All kind of books. Novels of romance, adventures, and horror. Poems—cheerful ones and dark ones. When Lynda grows up, she can read about anything: pain and happiness, darkness and light. She must learn of everything, though as a mother,

I hope she'll encounter only happiness. As for me, I don't resent the fear and the pain I experienced in the rainforest. If I hadn't been through it all, I might not appreciate every day, every minute, the way I do.

Those terrifying months in the rainforest were, in a way, a gift. Maybe it's true what they say, that without darkness, you can never truly appreciate the light.

Watching Tristan and Lynda on the porch, laughing on the phone, I slump in my favorite place in whole house: a rocking chair. Maybe it's all those months we spent in the plane, but I feel more comfortable sleeping in the rocking chair than in our bed. I can sit for hours at a time in it, reading stories to Lynda, or waiting for Tristan to come home from the hospital on the nights when he must work late. Over the rocking chair I throw a cover I made by sewing together patches. Each patch has a photo of Tristan and me, or the three of us. Each year I add a few patches to the blanket with pictures from moments that stand out. Tristan says if I continue like this, when we're old the blanket will be large enough to cover the whole house. I hope it will be. You can never have enough good memories. A light pain shoots through my left ankle. It happens now and then. But I smile. No matter what hardships life throws at us, I meet them with a smile. Because I will always remember a time when all I could hope for was one more breath, one more heartbeat. Now I have plenty of them.

And I intend to celebrate every single one.

Epilogue

Many years later

"Dr. Spencer," the nurse calls, her head visible through the cracked door, "we need you on the second floor."

"I'll be with you in a minute."

I close the file on my desk, trying to pull myself together. In over two decades of practicing medicine, I've grown immune to this type of situations. But there are always cases that get to me. And having known Dr. Tristan Bress and his family personally since I was a young woman makes it that much more difficult.

At the age of seventy, Aimee Bress was admitted to our hospital, where her husband had worked for many years before retiring. She had a severe case of viral respiratory disease. She was admitted three weeks ago, and her husband and daughter have been practically living outside her room ever since, though not allowed to see her. She has an exceptionally contagious form and it is very dangerous for Dr. Bress, whose age made him frail and prone to contract the virus.

Her condition worsened. Last night we informed Dr. Bress and his daughter that Aimee would not survive the night. When we told them they couldn't spend the night at her bedside due to the highly contagious nature of the virus, Dr. Bress asked his daughter to take him home. It seemed an odd request, not wanting to spend the night at the hospital, as close as possible to his wife. Before leaving, he took a little glass box out of his pocket. Taking out a circle made of old, decaying thread, he asked in a pleading voice, "Will you put this on my wife's finger next to her wedding ring?" Seeing a man who I had always associated with strength become so vulnerable immediately made me say a whispered "Yes." My weak answer didn't calm him. "Promise," he urged.

"I promise." I fulfilled my promise. His daughter returned alone to the hospital after dropping him off at home. Mrs. Bress died at four o'clock in the morning. Out of respect for having known and worked with Tristan Bress for years, I accompanied their daughter to her parents' home, to tell him.

We found Dr. Bress in a rocking chair, a blanket with layers upon layers covering him from his lap down.

His daughter thought he was asleep. But I knew better.

He had died.

In his hands, he was holding the glass box he had at the hospital. The box was empty, but a similar circle to the one he asked me to put on his wife's finger was on his, right next to his wedding ring. I thought I grew immune to everything over so many years, but I couldn't help shedding tears. Aimee Bress once told me about the time they spent in the Amazon rainforest. I remembered what those thread rings meant. I tried to hide my tears, but a closer inspection of the blanket on Dr. Bress's lap brought more tears. The blanket seemed to be made entirely out of patches with printed pictures of their family. Some photos must have been very old, because both Bresse's looked younger than I've ever seen them. It struck me that in all photos, no matter if they were young or not, they had that same look of intense love in their eyes that I was always secretly jealous of.

When the diagnostic of the cause of his death came—literally a broken heart—I expected it to be difficult to explain to their daughter. It's an unusual diagnostic, and one that people are sceptical about.

She smiled through tears. "My parents did love each other very much." Then she said a few words that I will carry with me for a very long time. "He loved her so much he never wanted to say goodbye to her. He wanted to leave with her."

The End

Other Books Available By Layla Hagen

Lost is a FREE prequel novella to *Lost in Us* and can be read before or after.

Whatever might help him forget his past and numb the pain, James has tried it all: booze, car races, fights, and then some. Especially women. College offers plenty of opportunities for everything. . . Especially when you have a trust fund to spend.

Serena spirals deeper and deeper into a hurricane of pain. But no matter how far she falls, there's no redemption from the overwhelming guilt.

Two souls consumed by their pasts fight to learn how to survive. But all hope seems to be lost.

Until they meet each other.

DOWNLOAD FOR FREE at all major retailers

Serena has learned to live with her past, locking her secrets and nightmares deep inside her. But when her boyfriend of six years abruptly leaves her, she's catapulted back into pain, nursing a broken heart. When indulging in mountains of chocolate doesn't work, Serena decides the best way to deal with her shattered heart is to indulge in something else. A rebound . . .

The night she swaps her usual Sprite for tequila, she meets James. The encounter is breathtaking.

Electrifying.

And best not repeated.

James is a successful entrepreneur in Silicon Valley. A man who has amassed a fortune by taking risks. A man who has shunned commitment completely, and still does. He's the exact opposite of Serena. But sometimes

opposites attract. Sometimes they give in to burning passion. Sometimes opposites are perfect for each other.

James is everything her damaged soul could want. His kisses are intoxicating, his touch out of this world. He makes her forget. He grants her peace from her pain. But as they grow closer, Serena discovers she isn't the only one with a past. James carries the scars of a past much darker than hers.

One that has left him damaged, hurt, and wary of love. A past that gives him the power to shatter her.

Now James and Serena must find a way to mend one another. Or risk losing each other forever.

All Jessica wants -as a college graduate — is to be a good girl. She landed the job of her dreams at a museum and is trying to eliminate temptations. No more short skirts (when she can help it). No wild parties. And no men.

She particularly excels at that last thing. . .

Until her path crosses Parker's. Again. Jessica remembers the last time their paths crossed very well. She was left with a seriously bruised ego. She knows it would be best to avoid him altogether. But the charming Brit makes it hard for her to elude his electrifying pull. He is as irresistible as he is captivating.

And enigmatic.

Because underneath the sleek Armani suit and the sweet British accent that makes her crave his touch, Parker isn't the perfect gentleman everyone thinks he is.

He's exactly what Jessica doesn't want, but desperately needs.

A bad, bad boy.

About the Author

My name is Layla Hagen and I am a New Adult Contemporary Romance author.

I fell in love with books when I was nine years old, and my love affair with stories continues even now, many years later.

I write romantic stories and can't wait to share them with the world.

And I drink coffee. Lots of it ;)

If you want to find out more about my current books and future releases, visit me at www.laylahagen.com

Acknowledgements

There are so many people who helped me fulfill the dream of publishing my novels, that I am utterly terrify I will forget to thank someone. If I do, please forgive me. Here it goes.

First, I'd like to thank my editors, Karen and Janet, whose hilarious comments and little smileys inserted along the manuscript made the editing process as enjoyable as the writing process. To all my beta readers (you know who you are): you have no idea how much your feedback helped me!! I am blessed to have such great people willing to take their time to help me. It goes without saying, but you improve my writing and stories vastly with your kindness.

Thank you also introducing me to Ari, who blew me away with her beautiful covers.

I want to thank every blogger and reader who took a chance with me as a new author and helped me spread the word. You have my most heartfelt gratitude. To my street team. . .you rock !!!

Last but not least, I would like to thank my family. I would never be here if not for their love and support. Mom, you taught me that books are important, and for that I will always be grateful. Dad, thank you for always being convinced that I should reach for the stars.

To my sister, whose numerous ahem. . .legendary

replies will serve as an inspiration for many books to come, I say thank you for your support and I love you, kid.

To my husband, who always, no matter what, believed in me and supported me through all this whether by happily taking on every chore I overlooked or accepting being ignored for hours at a time, and most importantly encouraged me whenever I needed it, I love you and I could not have done this without you.

Made in the USA
San Bernardino, CA
04 March 2015